THE ANACONDA OF Z

GAYNE C. YOUNG

SEVERED PRESS
HOBART TASMANIA

THE ANACONDA OF Z

Copyright © 2020 Gayne C. Young
Copyright © 2020 by Severed Press

WWW.SEVEREDPRESS.COM

ISBN: 978-1-922323-41-5

AMAZONIA 1922

The crocodilian exploded forward unleashing a geyser of black water that shot upwards of eight feet. The sudden burst of energy pulled tight the crossbow bolt embedded just behind the massive dragon's skull, snagging the barb tight against its inch-thick hide, releasing a rivulet of blood that shone purple in the half moon light. The beast dove beneath the surface of the Rio Negro and the force of the dive pulled floating debris and even small fish behind and into its wake.

Ross studied the beast in the darkness then called out, "Now!"

Kade pulled the rope and looped it around the forward cleat. The rope snapped tight and the wooden craft jerked forward, sending Kade backward and to the floor of the craft. He shot upward in embarrassment and held tight to the gunwales as the boat launched forward.

Ross laughed aloud at his mate's mishap then watched as the sisal rope strained tighter and tighter.

Then fell slack.

The boat drifted to a dead stop.

The river fell into a deafening silence.

Kade held his breath, afraid to break the moment or to draw attention to his being.

"He's gone under," Ross whispered to himself. He scanned the glass-still waters in every direction and clenched his teeth as he continued watching for signs. Something unknown called to him.

A feeling.

Experience.

He looked to his bare feet planted firmly in the half inch deep puddle in the bottom of the boat.

Did he feel something?

Or did he know something?

"He's under the boat," Ross mumbled. He turned to a pale faced Kade and smiled. "Hands in boy!"

Kade's eyes doubled in size. He jerked his hands toward his body just as four foot of jaws exploded from the water. The beast slammed its head against the boat, its jaws spread wide in search of the source of its torment. A bellowing moan brought forth the sudden smell of rot mixed with the coppery tinge of blood. Ross pulled the rusted .45 revolver from the holster at his hip. The leviathan dove forward and down. Its telephone pole-sized tail swung wildly then slammed against the side of the boat. The craft jerked forward and sped through the water as it was pulled by over 16 feet of black caiman.

Kade fell backward and against the floor once more and he cursed wildly in his native Portuguese as he righted himself. Ross holstered his pistol and fought to keep steady and stand erect in the ever-jostling craft.

"The size of that beast!" Ross exclaimed to the night. "That's a hell'uva lot a hide! A goddamn New York lady's whole set of luggage and then some!"

Kade smiled and nervously offered, "Is big" in broken English.

Ross stared ahead, watching the beast before the craft drive forward. The ridges of the crocodile's back cut through the water like a shark's dorsal fin and its tail undulated side to side in a frenzy of power and strength like some metronome confined to a fevered dream. The black figure dove yet again, and the boat slowed to a coast and then again to a dead halt. Kade put his hands in his armpits just in case and bounced his eyes back and forth to all sides of the boat, searching for the attack that he knew was coming.

It didn't.

There was only stillness.

The sounds of men in wait.

The water at the rope's length before the boat boiled.

Ross and Kade stared at the disturbance in anticipation of what was to come. The ink black water exploded with the force of a lightning strike. The black caiman's tail rose from the depths in a manner seemingly impossible. The tail pointed straight upward as if aiming at some distant constellation. The tail shot further upward and the water wretched forth a set of jaws that completely engulfed the crocodilian and held it aloft. A serpentine form towered from the water then arched backward in a blur of motion. Its jaws opened wider and the crocodile slid downward and into the dinosaur-sized snake.

"Mother of God!" Ross exclaimed.

"*Yacumama!*" Kade echoed. "*Yacumama!*"

Ross watched in disbelief as the last of the crocodile was swallowed. Shock gave way to panic as his eyes trained on the slack rope hanging from the snake's clenched jaws.

"Cut it!" Ross shouted. "Cut the rope!"

Kade reached for a machete sheathed along the interior wall of the boat.

"Do it boy! Cut the rope!" Ross screamed as he launched for the outboard motor's starter rope.

The snake homed in on the sudden noise and movement and snapped its head back in confusion. The rope jerked tight and the boat shot forward and upward and out of the water like a cork from a champagne bottle. Kade was thrown from the boat and into the water. The force of the impact knocked the breath from him. He fought to breathe but instead inhaled several mouthfuls of river water. He sunk below the surface and fought the depths in panic. He fought and clawed his way back to the surface. He broke through and into the darkness of the evening and simultaneously coughed and gasped for air.

He heard a pistol shot and spun around in the water just in time to see the snake plunge downward with mouth agape toward Ross in the boat. The beast's jaws closed tight around Ross' lower torso then raised its head and the human form within it toward the moon. Ross' legs kicked wildly in the air then disappeared into the creature's maw.

Kade shook in fright. He fought to scream, to vocalize his shock and disbelief but was unable to. The snake lowered its head in Kade's direction then dove beneath the water. Ross fought to gather his thoughts, fought to allow his brain to conjure a way out of the nightmare before him. A sudden rush of water engulfed him and the air was squeezed from his body. He felt himself rise from the water then realized he was trapped in the coils of the monstrous snake. The nightmare's head shot through the darkness and stopped less than a foot from Kade's face. Kade stared into the snake's coal black eyes and prayed that his death would be quick.

It was.

2.

Barrett Walker had lived the past 10 of his 33 years on Earth in the Brazilian rainforest. His journey to one of the last wild places on the planet began shortly after high school when he took a job on the railroad just outside his hometown of Meridian, Texas. The work was arduous and left him dead tired at the end of each day but helped him to pack 15 pounds of muscle onto his six-foot one-inch frame in less than three months. He laid his last railroad tie within view of the Port of Houston the following winter and decided then and there his fortune wouldn't be found in laying track.

He dropped his sledgehammer and walked toward the city and into the first bar he came to. He binged on tequila and beer and then on the pleasures of a Mexican lady the name of Lana with skin the color of soft caramel and breasts high and firm with youth. She only charged him for one trip to her bed and he spent the money he would have paid for a second rut to join in a poker game that resulted in him winning twice as much as he put down and receiving a partial ass kicking from a black man who towered three inches over him and outweighed him by more than 30 pounds.

The black man introduced himself as Big Jim on the tail end of an apology for flying off the handle at his poor poker skills. He complimented Barrett on his fighting ability and bought him a beer.

The pair moved from beer to tequila and together drank more than a bottle before the break of dawn.

"What you gonna do with your railway days behind you?" Big Jim asked with a heavy accent that Barrett had yet to place.

Barrett answered that he'd yet to think of an answer to that question but was open to suggestion. Big Jim thought then slurred that he was on good terms with the captain of the steam tramp *Scout* and that the company that owned the craft was always looking for good men. Big Jim explained the job and the duties required and of all the ports they would hit between Houston and Brazil. By the time the two men had killed the bottle of tequila, Barrett had agreed to the job and two days later found himself onboard the *Scout*.

Barrett took to the sea with little trouble, and to the monotony of the grunt work he was assigned, even better. Despite this ease, by the time he hit Brazil he was ready for a change. He kept his desire to change a secret from Big Jim during their week of shore leave during which the towering black man showed Barrett his home and introduced him to his wife and children. When Barrett did broach the subject of not wanting to return to the *Scout* with Big Jim, his shipmate said he understood and informed him that, "A good ol' Texas boy like yourself could make a time of it on the frontier."

Barrett listened intently as Big Jim told him of the wilds of Amazonia and of the money to be made there in rubber, timber, gold, meat, and hides. Over the next decade Barrett tried his hand at all these but found the hunting of snakes, lizards, and caiman for hides to be the best match for his skills and temperament. He hunted his way across Amazonia before settling after five years of travel in the frontier town of Messias near the Bolivian border.

Located on the Rio Abuna and translated as "Messiah" in English, the town of Messias was a haven for pirates and criminals, expatriates and fortune seekers, all of which relished spending their money in a town void of churches and schools and protected by a scant yet easily purchased law presence. The town offered each and every vice a man could think of for a price and vices as not yet condemned by society could be negotiated for as well. The center of vice in town was a riverfront bar known as Chorando Messias. There, patrons participated in and enjoyed anything a man could think of.

Barrett especially enjoyed their regular monkey fights.

Barrett ignored the roar of the crowd and instead gave the black howler monkey a hard study. The mangy primate known to all as Selvagem was missing an eye, had a body crisscrossed with scars of varying lengths and widths, and carried a tail that was more skin than fur.

"Selvagem's looking old," Barrett yelled over the crowd to the monkey's owner.

"Not old," the owner replied. "He bored. Tired of waiting to kill dog."

Barrett nodded then trained his eyes through the mass of people to the bulldog that sat at its owner's feet. It too was scared and carried the heavy burden of age and of a life spent fighting in and out of pits.

Barrett took a long pull on his flask of cachaça and yelled into the crowd, "I say he takes the dog in under five."

The crowd went wild and Barrett was bombarded with an array of odds. He listened intently then put $5 on the monkey to kill the dog in under four minutes at five to one odds.

An obese man covered in sweat pushed his way through the crowd and into the sand covered pit that sat surrounded by men and women of every size and color. The man drove a metal spike into the center of the ring with a 5-pound sledge and motioned for Selvagem and his owner to enter the ring. The owner complied and tied Selvagem's leash to the freshly driven metal rod. The owner left the ring and the monkey climbed up on the spike and perched upon it like some gargoyle found on the roof of a church constructed in medieval times. The obese man exited the pit and made his way to a small elevated platform that stood above the crowd.

"Ladies and gentlemen," the obese man yelled. "Welcome to the Crying Messiah!"

The crowd cheered and booed and some chanted for the fight to begin and others to bring out women instead.

"Tonight's main event features new challenger, Princess, taking on current and all-time champion, Selvagem!"

The crowd burst into cheers and screams, old bets were rescinded, and new ones made in a melee of sweaty, fevered excitement.

The obese man locked eyes with Selvagem's owner. The owner nodded in the affirmative and the bar owner looked to Princess' owner who nodded in the affirmative as well. The obese man spread his arms wide and decreed, "To the death!"

Princess' owner released his grip on the dog and the canine challenger tore forward at breakneck speed toward the still perched monkey. Selvagem lowered into a crouch and hissed, exposing a mouth full of glistening teeth. The dog lunged at the monkey and the black howler vaulted skyward. The simian turned in mid-air and came to land upon the dog's upper back. The crowd screamed in bliss or anguish depending upon his or her bets. The dog spun in a frenzied attempt to reach the monkey on its back and in the process got tangled in the small primate's leather leash. Selvagem grabbed the dog's left ear with both hands and pulled. The dog fell over and onto its side in an attempt to escape the pain the monkey was inflicting upon him.

Selvagem climbed on the dog's belly and sunk its teeth into the dog's neck. Princess yelped in pain as blood shot from her neck. The dog rolled over and Selvagem was knocked loose. Princess took the monkey's right leg in its mouth and bit down. The simian's bone snapped in two and the monkey howled in inhuman anguish. The crowd screamed louder and louder and stomped their feet and pumped their fists. Selvagem strafed his nails across the dog's eyes. Princess shrieked in pain and released her grip on the monkey's leg. The black howler sunk his teeth into the dog's throat and bit downward, releasing a surging fountain of arterial blood. Some in the crowd relished in this and cheered and jumped up and down, rejoicing, while others booed and angrily threw money at those that they had placed a bet with. The dog spasmed once then fell dead.

"The winner and still champion," the obese bar owner yelled over the crowd. "Selvagem!"

3.

Neal Coldwell found the Crying Messiah to be about the most horrid place he'd ever seen. The moment he stepped through its front doors and onto the roughhewn plank floor, he was concerned for his health and safety. The smell of cheap booze, stale beer, rank perfume, blood, vomit, and body odor was overwhelming. The air was a fog of cigar, cigarette, and hookah smoke. The people within appeared to be the dregs of society. The populace was a mixture of Anglos, Indians, Brazilians, and those so worn looking that their nationality and race were unidentifiable. The hotel clerk had assured Neal that the Crying Messiah, or the Chorando Messias as he called it, was the most popular establishment in town and his best bet to find Barrett Walker. Not seeing anyone who fit Barrett's description, Neal made his way through the maze of tables and patrons to the bar.

"Excuse me," Neal said to the dark-skinned bartender.

Neal took the man for some type of local Indian. His hair was blacker than coal and his dark skin a mosaic of tribal tattoos and raised ceremonial whelps.

"What?" the bartender angrily shot back.

"I'm looking for Barrett Walker."

"So?"

Neal fished some bills from his pants pocket and handed them across the bar.

"So, I was hoping you could point me in the right direction."

The gruff bartender pocketed the money and pointed to the rear of the establishment.

"Outside!" he blurted. "Monkey fight."

"Excuse me, did you say…"

"Monkey fight. Outside. Barrett's there."

Neal nodded and made his way to the rear of the bar. He exited to a large courtyard illuminated by naked bulbs spliced into wires high above the crowd. A small round arena of some kind was surrounded by people of every color and creed. Neal scanned the crowd until he spotted a man that fit the hotel clerk's description of the man he was seeking.

Barrett was a tall man with broad shoulders and a barrel chest. He had dirty blonde hair that was partially slicked back on top, but razor shorn on the sides. His face carried at least three days of stubble and his blue chambray shirt and his khaki pants were faded and weathered. The Colt 1911 on his hip looked old and weathered as well and even at the distance at which Neal stood, he could see the bluing had worn thin or had vanished from the metal completely. Neal made his way through the tightly pressed crowd and to within handshake distance of Barrett.

Barrett shoved a handful of cash into his pockets and put an unlit stub of a cigar in his mouth. He struck a match across the top of the pistol in his holster and held the flame to his cigar. He was enjoying the last bit the cigar had to offer when he noticed an odd man walking toward him.

The man was tall and lean and despite being impeccably dressed in a tailored linen suit, looked extremely uncomfortable. He walked uneasily through the crowd in an odd gait that reminded Barrett of a kitten taking its first steps.

"Barrett Walker," Neal excitedly exclaimed as he held his hand out before him in greeting.

"Who's asking?" Barrett inquired on a puff of cigar smoke.

"Dr. Neal Coldwell, American Museum of Natural History."

Barrett stood stoic.

He blew another puff of smoke.

"I was wondering if I could buy you a drink," Neal continued.

"I ain't into that," Barrett answered.

"Into what?"

"Into whatever you're expecting to get in return for buying me a drink."

Neal was taken aback.

He fumbled his words.

"No…I…I just want to talk to you. I'm a herpetologist, a scientist that studies reptiles and amphibians. Reptiles mostly. I specialize in snakes. I'd like to get your opinion on indigenous snakes."

"Conversation like that sounds like it'll take more than one drink."

"It does?"

"The way I drink it will."

Neal smiled then offered, "Sounds like a plan."

Barrett nodded and led Neal through the dissipating crowd to the inside of the bar. Barrett took a table in the rear corner, killed his stub of a cigar in the center ashtray, and took a fresh one from his pocket. He bit the end off and spat it upon the floor. Neal sidestepped the spit cigar end and sat. Barrett motioned for a waitress to come over and Neal watched as a short Indian woman with a round figure in bare feet approached them.

"What?" the waitress barked.

"Bring us a bottle. Two glasses of ice."

The waitress left without acknowledging Barrett's request.

"Is everyone that works here like that?" Neal asked.

"Like what?"

"I don't know." Neal thought for a moment. "Rude. As if they hate working here."

"Yeah," Barrett laughed. "It seems to be one of the requirements for employment."

The waitress returned and placed a bottle and two glasses on the table with a heavy thud.

"No ice!" she announced. "Who pay?"

Barrett poured himself a drink and pointed to Neal. The waitress held her hand out and Neal placed a few bills upon it.

"More!" the waitress exclaimed.

"It costs that much?" Neal questioned in surprise.

"Tip!" the waitress barked in response.

Neal nodded and gave the waitress another two bills. The waitress stomped off on bare feet and Barrett pushed a half full glass across the table to Neal.

"Have you had cachaça yet?"

"No. But it's like rum, yes? Made from sugar cane."

"Yeah and this ain't the good stuff."

Barrett downed his shot and poured another. Neal drank half of his shot and tried not to let his face contort into the image of shock he felt at the drink's strength. He forced the drink down his throat then pushed the glass across the table to Barrett who poured him another. Barrett slid the just poured shot across the table to Neal then lit his new cigar.

"We're one drink in and you haven't told me what you want," Barrett offered.

"I'm a herpetologist with the Museum of Natural History."

"You told me that."

Neal shook his head in nervousness.

"I did...I did. I apologize. I'm just nervous finally getting to...No. I'm excited at the possibility of what lies ahead," Neal began again. "I've told you I'm a herpetologist, but I didn't tell you that I specialize in South American snakes."

Barrett exhaled a series of small smoke rings.

Neal saw this as a lack of interest on Barrett's part and changed direction in his approach. He calmed himself and began anew.

"In 1907, while mapping the border between Brazil and Bolivia, British explorer Colonel Percy Fawcett and his men came across an anaconda of epic proportions."

Neal quickly retrieved a small worn leather journal from the interior pocket of his suit jacket. He frantically leafed through the pages until he found what he was looking for. He read, "We were drifting easily along on the sluggish current...when almost under the bow there appeared a triangular head and several feet of undulating body. It was a giant anaconda. I sprang for my rifle as the creature began to make its way up the bank, and hardly waiting to aim, smashed a .44 soft-nosed bullet into its spine, ten feet below the wicked head…"

"I've heard the story before," Barrett interrupted.

Neal returned the worn journal to his pocket.

"The snake Colonel Fawcett wrote of was over 60 feet long."

"Bullshit," Barrett declared.

Neal's face winced in disappointment.

Barrett downed another shot of cachaça then refilled his glass.

"I know the story. It's bullshit."

"No, I assure you it's accurate. I've corresponded with Colonel Fawcett personally. He further detailed the encounter."

"It's bullshit," Barrett reiterated on a puff of smoke.

Neal's disappointment grew to anger. He was angry that Barrett wouldn't listen to him and that he wouldn't let him finish what he traveled so far to say.

"And anacondas don't get that big," Barrett continued.

"What's the biggest you've ever seen? In the wild?" Neal angrily shot back.

"I took a 24-footer in a tributary of the Rio Abuna some three years back and that's four feet longer than the next runner-up."

"I know for a fact they can get bigger than that and I know Fawcett was telling the truth."

Neal angrily poured a drink down his throat and slid his empty glass across the table as if daring Barrett to pour him another. Barrett smirked and poured Neal another drink. He slid it back across the table then raised his glass. Neal raised his in response and they clinked glasses, then drank.

"Look, Doc," Barrett began again, once more, yet this time with a more respectful tone. "I'm sure what I don't know 'bout snakes could fill volumes, but I think snakes the size you're talking about went the way of the dinosaur."

"Maybe in the areas you've hunted."

"And even if Fawcett was telling the truth, which he ain't because he's a reckless nut job that will end up on the wrong end of an arrow someday, that incident was over a decade ago. Snakes don't live that long. Especially snakes that have been shot with a .44."

"Fawcett told me that the snake was still alive. That he believes his team merely stunned the snake when they shot it and that the snake went rigid and slid back into the river."

Barrett took a puff on his cigar, found it dead, and relit it.

"And snakes can live a very long time," Neal continued.

"What's your bottom line on all this?" Barrett interrupted on a puff of smoke. "Why are you arguing this with me?"

"I want to hire you. I want you to take me to the Rio Negro."

"That's down in Bolivia."

"To the area where Fawcett…"

"That's unexplored territory. No one's been there but Fawcett and his team barely made it out of there alive. And snakes were the least of their problems."

"You'll be compensated."

"No money's worth dying for."

"Payment for the expedition upfront and rights to everything we discover outside of proof of Fawcett's snake is yours. Your financial gain could be enormous. You'd be set up for life. Especially down here."

"I'm not interested."

"The money you'd make…"

"Decision's final."

Neal's crushing disappointment was interrupted by a sudden swelling of the bar crowd. Neal directed his attention toward a swarm of people entering the bar from the rear. The crowd was following a man who held something aloft.

"Is that monkey wearing a cast?" Neal asked.

Barrett stood and clapped, then offered, "That's Selvagem. He got damn near bit in half in the fight. Good to see him patched up."

"Fight?"

"Yeah. He took on a bulldog. Killed it in under four minutes."

"People fight monkeys against dogs here?" Neal said in disbelief. "To the death?"

Barrett nodded in the affirmative.

"I've never seen such a thing."

"Where are you from?"

"New York."

"They got monkeys there?"

"No."

"Well, there's your answer why you haven't."

4.

Neal sat alone in the small restaurant of his hotel, picking unenthusiastically at a plate of cold beans and rice. His head was throbbing from drinking the night before and this morning he now understood why the name cachaça was slang for "retard." He felt retarded for drinking so much of it the night before and felt as though he was far dumber than he was before he had taken his first drink of it. Cachaça was powerful stuff.

Neal took a forkful of food then put it down and drank some more water instead, then wiped his sweaty brow with a napkin. He had yet to adapt to the high heat and unreal humidity of Amazonia in the past few days and it was taking a brutal toll on his body. The hotel clerk noticed Neal's lack of interest in his food and left his desk to see what, if anything, the American needed. Jose had found that weak Americans such as Neal tipped more if they were babied enough.

"You like something else to eat? Something different?" Jose asked.

Embarrassment washed over Neal's face. He felt pathetic and he apparently looked it as well.

"No, it was very good," Neal assured Jose. "I'm just not that hungry."

Jose studied the pale man that sat before him. He was green in the gills and sweating like a pig.

"You've got two choices," Jose explained.

Neal was taken aback and a sudden nervousness ran the length of his spine.

"You can have some coffee and suffer throughout the day or you can have, as I hear you Americans call it, some hair of the dog."

Neal smiled. "Is it that obvious?"

"Cachaça's a bitch for the uninitiated, especially if you're not used to the heat yet."

"I'm definitely not that."

"Then a little cachaça in some fruit juice coming right up."

Neal didn't respond.

He couldn't.

Jose left with his plate before he could.

Neal finished his water and again wiped his brow. He ran once more through the meeting with Barrett the night before. He tried to recall every word he had said and Barrett's every response in an effort to understand how he failed to convince the man to lead his expedition into the unknown and in search of a monster from another time. This was more than a snake of legend. This was an animal whose capture and study could re-write what science knew about snakes, reptiles, and the ecosystems that supported such.

"Try this," Jose offered, placing a tall glass before Neal.

"What is it?" Neal asked, holding the glass up in study.

"Mango juice with a little cachaça. Not much. Just enough."

Neal tried the drink then smiled.

"Very nice."

"Nurse that and you'll be feeling better in no time."

Neal nodded and offered thanks then said, "I didn't have much luck with Mr. Walker last night. I'd like to try again. Any idea where I might find him this evening?"

"The Crying Messiah."

"That same ghastly bar? The one that features monkeys fighting to the death?"

"Yes. And I heard Selvagem won again last night. Did you see it?"

Neal stammered slightly in an attempt not to offend the man's interest in simian combat sports. "Uh…No…I got there too late."

"I heard it was a good fight. Really wish I'd made it over there."

Neal tried to put gladiatorial monkeys out of his head.

"Mr. Walker will be there? Again, tonight, you think?" Neal asked.

"The man basically lives there when he's in town. Unless he's shacked up with some woman that is."

5.

"Turtle eggs?" Barrett scoffed on an exhale of cigar smoke.

"Yeah," Doyle said, dropping his empty shot glass on the bar. He gestured to the bartender for another drink then returned his attention to Barrett. "I got me a Chinese up in Porto Velho, pays really well for them. He pickles 'em with Chink spices or some such nonsense and ships them back to China. This beach my boy Paulo knows about, he says he's seen more than a hundred turtles at a time on shore dropping sacks."

Barrett nodded with understanding and killed his beer.

"Get him another one," Doyle instructed the barkeeper who was in the process of pouring a shot down the bar.

Barrett gave Doyle an appreciative look and continued feigning interest in the man's story.

"There's money to be made in this for you too. Lots I figure," Doyle explained.

Barrett held his opinion and instead took his beer from the bartender. He took a long pull on the bottle then scowled at the drink's warmth and asked Doyle what he was offering in the way of eggs.

"The eggs is mine," Doyle quickly explained. "But I'll split the money from the hides and shells."

"You ever clean a turtle, Doyle?" Barrett scoffed.

"Can't say that I've had that pleasure," Doyle laughed.

"It's not worth the doing. Hide prices don't make up for the time involved and I've never met a buyer for turtle shells."

"Do you know these turtles I'm talking about?"

Barrett took another long pull on his beer and scowled again at its temperature.

"They've got shells twice the size of a fat woman's ass," Doyle continued. "Every high society poser up in New York City would kill to have one of them cleaned and varnished, hanging in their homes."

Barrett cracked a smile and nodded.

"And it ain't like all that much work on your part. Throw you some booze money at a few Indians for hire and you got yer' ass a turtle shell cleaning crew."

Doyle took a drink then looked to Barrett for affirmation but saw none. He continued, nonetheless.

"I'm short of the upfront money is why I'm bringing this to you, you see. I got all my money tied up in the egg portion of this here endeavor."

"An endeavor!" Neal suddenly exclaimed aloud. He stepped in between where Barrett and Doyle leaned at the bar and held a finger aloft to alert the bartender. The bartender saw this, frowned in contempt and returned instead to chipping some dried foreign substance from a drinking glass.

"Who the hell is you coming up in here, jumping into the middle of my business?" Doyle bellowed.

Neal took a small step back at the question and Doyle took a step forward. Barrett killed his beer and offered, "He's with me. Forgot he was supposed to meet me here."

"Where's he from that he's got the manners he's throwing my direction?!"

"New…York," Neal stammered, holding out his hand in greeting. "Name is…Dr. Neal Coldwell."

Doyle slapped Neal's hand away and declared, "Like I give a big fat shit who you are!"

Barrett raised from his leaning position at the bar. Doyle saw this and understood the movement's meaning. He stepped back and said, "Tend to your business with Mr. New York manners here. I'll catch ya' later."

"Yeah, let's talk business." Barrett nodded and led Neal to the same table the two men had sat at the night before.

"Thanks," Barrett said as he took a seat.

"Thanks for what?" Neal inquired as he took a seat of his own.

"You saved me from talking turtles with that guy."

"Turtles?" Neal exclaimed with a tinge of excitement. "What about them?"

"Nothing I want to talk about."

"Good because I'd rather talk about…"

"What you want?" a stern voice interrupted. Neal turned in his chair to see the same round Indian waitress from the night before.

"Beer," Barrett answered. "One that ain't body temperature like the one I just had."

"Cold beer extra!" the waitress barked. "You know that. And no more credit for you."

"Give me a cold one and I don't need credit," Barrett explained. "The doc here is paying."

Neal smiled and nodded in agreement. He stood and took a wad of bills from his pocket. He gave them to the waitress and said, "Cold beers and keep them coming."

Neal sat then watched with a sudden queasiness as the waitress pushed the bills into her long, deep cavernous cleavage. The waitress turned to leave and Neal returned his attention toward Barrett.

"I think she likes you," Barrett joked.

"Yes. Lovely girl."

"Her sister's not bad," Barrett added.

The waitress returned with the beers. She angrily placed them on the table without saying a word and left.

"Cheers," Neal offered, and the men clinked bottles.

Barrett took a short pull on his beer and, finding the temperature far more to his liking, downed half of it before coming up for air. He relit his cigar and exhaled a grayish cloud that rose and spun wildly in the currents created by the bar's many ceiling fans.

"As I was saying," Neal began again.

"I'm not going," Barrett interrupted.

"From what I've heard," Neal tried once more. "You came down here to make your fortune. This is your chance for that fortune. This is your chance for a lifetime of good fortune. Books. Speaking engagements…"

"Ain't you here for the same reason?" Barrett interrupted on an exhale of smoke.

"No. My fortune lies in academia. And the idea that one day those who come behind me will expand on what is known thanks to what I discovered. What we discovered."

Barrett took another long pull on his beer then motioned for another. Neal guzzled his beer in an effort to catch up.

"I'm not trying to sell you some holier than thou ideal," Neal continued. "You and I are the same. We both want something out of life and we're each in a position to help the other one achieve it."

The waitress brought another two beers and placed them up on the table. She took Barrett's empty then reached for Neal's.

"I'm not quite through," Neal explained.

"You drink like a girl," the waitress insulted.

Neal looked the barefoot block of an Indian waitress slowly up and down. He saw in her an opportunity to win Barrett's favor, to show the frontiersman that he was far from just an intellectual egghead with a passion for snakes. He decided to take a chance.

"What would you possibly know about being a girl?" Neal insulted.

The waitress' face tightened.

Barrett cracked a smile.

The Indian pulled back her arm and drove her fist forward and into Neal's chin with all her might. Neal flew backward, from his chair and to the floor.

Barrett burst into laughter.

The waitress dropped on top of Neal and began pummeling him. Barrett rushed to pull the waitress off the herpetologist. A crowd gathered around the melee and some cheered and others placed bets. Barrett pulled the monster of a barmaid upward and pushed her towards the bar.

"Go on!" Barrett instructed. "You're gonna wear yourself out beating on him like that."

Barrett turned and gave Neal a hand up then slapped him on the back.

"Show's over," Barrett announced to the crowd. "She won."

The crowd reluctantly dissipated, and Neal and Barrett sat. Barrett smiled and raised his beer in congratulations. Neal matched him and the two men laughed.

Barrett gestured for Neal to wipe his nose. Neal did and came away with a small amount of blood on his hand. He wiped this from his hand then cleaned his nose with a small handkerchief.

Barrett internally admitted he'd been wrong about Neal. Although a professor, he was far from an intellectual bore. He could hold his own in the world and wasn't shy about what he wanted from it. He had a good sense of humor and he was the kind of man who would let a waitress kick his ass in order to prove all of the aforementioned to another man. But taking that man into the unknown was another matter altogether.

"Tell me again what Fawcett said about the snake," Barrett began.

Excitement washed over Neal's face. Barrett saw this and did his best to abate it.

"I'm just asking. Don't get too excited."

"Of course," Neal said in understanding.

Neal told of how Colonel Fawcett had written him about the massive serpent during one of his supply stops in his search for the

Lost City of Z. Neal offered to read the letter, but Barrett insisted he not.

"Just give me the high points," Barrett exclaimed on a new drink of beer.

Neal continued.

He said that Colonel Fawcett stated that he had no doubt the snake had only been stunned by the gunshot, that the weapons his men had at their disposal were subpar at best, and that the shot released no blood into the water. Because of this, Fawcett and his party surmised that the serpent had merely been stunned and likely returned to the safety of the depths to avoid any further pain.

Fawcett had also written that the area where his group had encountered the snake produced a plethora of evidence of extremely large serpents. The expedition had found spoor and shed skins and slides or track channels that showed movement between the river in the jungle.

"That whole area is a no man's land," Barrett interrupted. "There's a thousand stories about the evil that lurks there. How it's a place where the Gods reign. It's a land of perpetual darkness. All kinds of hocus pocus nonsense."

"*Yacumama*," Neal said. "The Mother of Water."

Barrett took a long pull on his cigar and exhaled.

"Yeah, the Mother of the Waters. That's one of the stories," Barrett mumbled.

He left the discussion of Gods and instead returned to the reality of men.

"I don't know of anyone that's gone there and come back to tell of it. Other than Fawcett that is. My main competition in caiman hides set out there three months ago. He never came back."

Neal leaned forward.

"All the more reason to go," he said.

"Oh really?" Barrett said sarcastically.

"Yes! Think of the discoveries to be found there. That no one has brought back."

Barrett ignored the professor's excitement and instead studied the two uniformed policemen walking across the bar in his direction. Barrett knew the two men but had never seen them look so intent and had never seen them in uniform outside of their portraits that hung in the jail.

The two small Indians crossed the bar in heavy determination. They zeroed in on Barrett's table and made their way to it in haste.

"Oh shit," Barrett mumbled.

He killed his beer and eased back in his chair and tried to look as if he was ready for a friendly conversation.

The two policemen approached the table and the larger of the two tossed a rusty set of handcuffs on the table. The sound of the bracelets hitting the wood served as a call to action and the packed bar circled the table in fevered excitement of what was hopefully to come.

"You to put on, Walker," the larger of the two Indians instructed in broken English. "You come with us."

"Now wait a minute Ari," Barrett tried.

The cop that had dropped the cuffs scowled and furiously barked, "I not Ari. He Ari."

"Oh yeah," Barrett smiled. "You're the one whose name I can never pronounce."

The man didn't bother to enunciate his name for Barrett.

He instead drew a revolver that was far rustier than the handcuffs he had dropped on the table and pointed it at Barrett.

"Put on!" the man barked, gesturing to the shackles.

Barrett took the cuffs into his hands.

"If you insist."

6.

The two cops threw Barrett into the ancient jail cell and watched in sadistic glee as he smashed against the far wall. Barrett's nose crashed into the concrete structure, sending a small trickle of blood down and over his lip. He spat the foreign substance from his mouth and spun around in a boil of anger.

"What is all this shit?!" Barrett bellowed.

His answer came in the form of Chief Marcos Silva.

The chief stood smiling in the doorway of the cell with his shoulders back and his chest pushed out in an effort to look bigger and in better shape than he actually was. In truth, he was a poor physical specimen standing just five foot four inches tall and carrying an extra 30 pounds around the middle. The hair upon his head was thinning and receding and the strands growing from his nostrils thick and black. He entered the cell with a swagger that announced that he and he alone was in charge.

"Silva!" Barrett almost sang in smart-assed enthusiasm. "Thank God you're here."

The chief of police scowled.

"Your boys here are really confused. They must think I'm someone else," Barrett continued. "And I gotta say, they haven't been treating me very nicely."

The chief's scowl deepened. His eyes squinted and his jaw tightened.

The two cops saw this and held Barrett by the shoulders. Barrett protested physically but it was to no avail. His hands were still cuffed before him and the two Indians were too strong. The chief walked forward to in front of Barrett.

"Don't do anything you're gonna regret now, Silva." Barrett's voice trembled slightly.

The chief smiled.

Barrett smiled.

The two cops smiled.

The chief gently patted Barrett's cheek three times in quick succession and decreed, "Can't mess up that pretty face."

The chief's smile grew.

The cops' smiles grew.

Barrett's eyes questioned what was next.

"Turn him around," the chief laughed.

The two cops did as instructed. Barrett tightened every muscle in his being. The chief reared back and drove all the weight in his body through his fist and into Barrett's left kidney. Barrett winced in excruciating pain. It took all he had not to scream. The chief reared back once more and delivered a blow to Barrett's right kidney. Barrett fell to his knees. The two cops pulled Barrett up and the chief delivered two more kidney blows. The cops released Barrett and he fell to the concrete floor in a worthless heap.

7.

Doyle drunkenly stumbled through the old engine parts, rotted nets, broken oars, littered trash, and general refuse that was his yard and to the steps of his home. Like most homes in Messias that were situated along the river, Doyle's was built upon stilts to avoid the heavy floodwaters that were common in the rainy season. Doyle paused at the bottom of the stairs to finish his beer. He killed the drink and tossed it over his shoulder and into the yard where it hit an old boat motor and shattered. Doyle belched loudly and climbed the mildew painted stairs until he reached the landing of the wrap-around porch. He wheezed in partial exhaustion, lit a cigarette, then continued onward and to the deck.

"Paulo!" Doyle coughed. "Paulo, where the hell are you?"

No answer came.

Doyle walked to the rear of his porch and to the hammock Paulo usually slept in. Not finding the Indian there, he yelled his name once more.

"Paulo! Dammit, where are you?"

Doyle took a heavy pull on his cigarette and in the glow of the flaring tip saw Paulo walking from the darkness and toward him.

"Where the hell you been?" Doyle barked. "I've been calling you going on 10 minutes straight now."

Paulo ignored what he knew to be an incredible exaggeration of time and instead awaited the next thing to spill out of his boss' mouth.

"Grab me a beer," Doyle insisted. "Then get out here. We've got some planning to do."

Paulo nodded and made his way around the porch to the front of the house. He entered the filthy living quarters, grabbed a bottle of beer from a wooden case sitting upon the floor, and returned to find Doyle parked on a partially rotted crate that sat on the porch. Paulo opened the beer and gave it to Doyle who quickly downed a third of it in one swig. Doyle belched, killed his cigarette, and ground the butt into the wooden deck with his boot.

"The turtle job is off," Doyle began. "I got something better lined up."

Paulo stood listening.

Doyle took another slug of beer and continued.

"Heard that hot shot Barrett talking with some shit for manners reptile doctor about one hell'uva snake."

Paulo showed no change in emotion.

"They called it a yarma-ulke. Yacu-you-mama. Yamaka. No," Doyle suddenly corrected himself. "That last one's a Jewish thing."

Paulo's face washed with a sudden anxiety. Doyle saw this and questioned the change with a look. Paulo swallowed and strained to find the words to convey his thoughts.

"What the hell's wrong with you? You look like you had an umbrella opened in your ass," Doyle questioned.

Paulo didn't understand most of the question or comment but did understand the lack of concern behind it.

"You no can hunt *Yacumama.*"

"What the hell kind of snake is that?" Doyle inquired. "It was loud in the bar. I didn't hear everything about the snake. Just the size and where it lives."

"*Yacumama* is the Mother of Water. She carved rivers with body. She much big."

Doyle studied Paulo's concern for a moment then burst into heavy laughter. He lit a new cigarette and took in a deep lungful to calm his guffaws.

"That sounds like a load of crap," Doyle offered. "A snake so big it carved the rivers with its might."

"It true."

"It's true that we're heading out tomorrow after that thing," Doyle mocked.

Paulo's mask of anxiety grew.

"Where? Where to go?"

"Down into Bolivia. Where the Abuna meets the Negro."

Paulo thought of the place his boss was describing. It was a place of myth and reality, a place so thick and impenetrable that the few that had ventured there had never returned.

"That place is no too good."

Doyle laughed and said, "It will be good for me if we get that snake. Real good."

8.

Neal found the police chief's office to be almost as disgusting as the Crying Messiah. The entire building smelled of urine and stale cigarette smoke, vomit and rot. The walls were water stained and moldy and the tile floor cracked and streaked with filth. Neal entered the building and walked to the counter that stood constructed of old crates and mismatched lumber. Chief Silva came from a small desk in the back corner of the building to stand at the counter opposite Neal.

The chief didn't acknowledge Neal in any way, shape, or form. He simply stood at the counter staring forward and into oblivion. After a time, Neal politely inquired, "Do you speak English?"

"Of course," the chief replied with not a trace of emotion.

"Good!" Neal exclaimed. "That will make things much easier."

Neal paused for some type of reply either vocal or facial, but none came.

"I understand you are holding my friend, Barrett Walker," Neal tried once more.

The chief's face held stoic.

"If that's the case," Neal continued, "might I inquire as to the charge."

The chief exploded in a fit of rage.

"The charge is he slept with my wife! More than once!" the chief spat. "On more than one occasion! And in more than one position!"

Neal stood dumbstruck.

The chief continued.

"I know that my wife is of poor character and that she is crazy. But I prefer she not sleep with the likes of Barrett."

"Yes. A man such as yourself, of such high regard in the community."

"What do you want?!" The chief's bellow shook the makeshift counter.

"I want to get Barrett out of your hair. To take him far from here and away from your wife."

Calmness washed over the chief's face and his eyes showed interest in Neal's wants.

"Of course, I know you can't simply release a prisoner, not without bail that is."

"You would be correct in that regard," the chief said, returning to his earlier stoic demeanor.

"Would $50 cover his bail and processing fees?"

"American?"

"Yes. American money."

The chief didn't respond.

He simply held out his hand.

9.

The Barrett that stood in the filth ridden street outside of the police station was not the man Neal had seen the night before. This version of Barrett looked beaten and downtrodden, like some caricature of his prior self. His face was pale and sheened in sweat, his eyes were glassy and distant, and his hair a tasseled mess that stood on end in almost every direction. Looking Barrett up and down, Neal was at a loss of words. He didn't know what to say to a man he had only recently met who seemed so completely broken.

Luckily, Barrett spoke first.

"I need a drink."

Neal smiled and accommodated Barrett by taking him across town and back to the Crying Messiah. Even at that early morning hour, the bar was filled with a fog of smoke. Neal gazed through the smog to see customers passed out on the floor or sleeping with their heads upon tables. The air was filled with the sounds of wheezing and snoring, of the movement of rusty ceiling fans high above, and of the distant shuffling of bottles.

Barrett crossed the floor in obvious pain and gently lowered himself into his favorite chair. Neal watched this and made his way to the bar. He returned to the table a short time later with two dirty glasses and a bottle of cachaça. Barrett took the bottle and upended it. Neal watched as bubbles rose through the alcohol and to the top of the upside-down bottle. Barrett dropped the bottle from his face and poured two glasses. He slid one glass across the table to Neal who caught it in the palm of his hand. Barrett lifted his glass and Neal mirrored the action.

"Thanks," Barrett solemnly declared.

The two men clinked glasses and drank. Barrett placed his glass on the table and bemused, "The first time I got that dame undressed, I looked her naked body over and said, 'This is gonna be worth the consequences.'"

Barrett paused to rub his lower back.

He continued. "Now I'm not so sure."

Neal began to form a question, but it was answered before it could leave his lips.

"The chief went to town on my kidneys like a fat kid on a piñata full of candy."

Neal smiled at the explanation.

Barrett poured another round of drinks and gestured towards the one he had poured for himself.

"That and every other liquid that comes out of me for the next few weeks is gonna have some blood in it."

Barrett's words sent a shiver up Neal's spine. He couldn't imagine such pain.

Barrett lifted his glass once more in celebration.

"Seriously though, thank you for getting me out of there. I owe you one."

Neal coughed down his drink then declared with a devilish grin, "Yes, you do owe me. Quite a bit in fact."

In a matter of seconds, Barrett's face flew through a myriad of emotions. The muscles in his face contorted through shock, anger, acceptance, hatred, and utter disbelief.

"What?" Barrett questioned.

"You do owe me."

Barrett knew where Neal was going. He exploded.

"You son of a..."

"I saved your life," Neal interrupted.

Barrett tried to calm himself.

"I paid a very large bail."

"How much?" Barrett snapped.

"Fifty US dollars."

Barrett sighed heavily in disbelief and anger.

Fifty dollars was a huge amount of money. He could probably scrape together most of the cash but it would leave him financially destitute.

Neal continued.

"And I had to promise to get you out of town. Chief Silva was very adamant on this point. I don't know what would befall you if you were to push your luck by staying in town."

Barrett knew.

He'd most likely be taken back to jail and beaten again and again until the chief's anger at his sleeping with his wife abated. How long that would take was anybody's guess. The chief was known to be temperamental. And he did enjoy watching people suffer.

Barrett angrily assessed his situation and decided to make the best of it.

"You offered half," Barrett began. "I assume that's still on the table?"

"Half what?"

"Half of everything we discover," Barrett angrily shot back.

Neal nodded.

Barrett continued.

"I want double my standard guiding fee plus all expenses. I'm talking porters, fuel, new guns, arms, ammunition, cigars, booze, clothing, everything. And none of that comes out of my share."

Neal was ecstatic. He could hardly wait to enter the unexplored to search for what he knew would certainly prove to be a discovery of monstrous proportions, both physically and literally.

"And the bribe you paid to get me out of the clink," Barrett continued. "That was a freebie."

"Agreed. On all points," Neal assured Barrett.

Barrett frowned then poured and killed another shot of cachaça.

"You know the chances of us making it out of that territory alive, let alone finding anything remotely resembling your snake, are extremely slim," Barrett warned.

"I have full faith in your capabilities," Neal promised.

Neal reached inside his linen suit coat to retrieve a cigar. He handed it to Barrett who received it with a smile. Barrett bit off the end of the cigar and spat on the floor then lit the smoke and eased back into his chair. The movement quickly reminded him of his pain and he grimaced slightly. He took another few puffs then asked Neal if he had any field experience to his name whatsoever.

Neal told how he had been on collecting trips in the Yucatán Jungle of Mexico and the Everglades of Florida, the swamps of coastal Texas and the Barrier Islands of South Carolina. When Barrett said all of those expeditions would seem like child's play when compared to the force of nature they would most likely experience in the territory they planned to explore, Neal assured Barrett he knew how to hold his own in the wild and that he had faced life and death many times during his collecting trips.

Neal related the story of the time he was in the Everglades and how an assistant of his had both legs snapped like twigs when a 10-foot alligator's tail swung into them while trying to subdue the animal. The crocodilian spun around to take a bite out of the broken man but Neal had been quicker on the draw with his pistol than the alligator was on his attack. During that same trip, Neal had gotten bitten below the knee by a water moccasin that measured almost six feet in length. The bite had nearly killed him as had a sudden hurricane that did all it could to keep him and his team from making it back to civilization.

Barrett listened to Neal's stories and agreed that surviving such events gave Neal more clout in his eyes but then warned, "You ain't seen nothing yet."

10.

Paulo retrieved his cousin, Angel, and together the two Indians made their way to the home of Doyle Bannon. The sun was just coming up and its early morning rays shone down upon the Rio Abuna, casting the fog that sat upon it in an eerie rust color. During the long walk from Angel's home, Paulo explained that the trip Doyle had planned was a dangerous one but one that, given the man's ignorance, laziness, and constant state of near drunkenness, wasn't likely to get very far. Paulo added that they would be paid a daily rate regardless of the journey's outcome.

Paulo and Angel arrived to find Doyle doing his best to load supplies into his 20-foot boat. The vessel was old and the wood it was crafted from rotting, but the craft was wide and stable and traveled easily through shallow water. The small outboard motor was cantankerous but easily maintained by Paulo.

"About time," Doyle barked. He walked up the small dock and to the two Indians. He looked to Angel and said, "You ready to make some money?"

Angel nodded and smiled.

Doyle turned to Paulo and laughed, "Always the talker your cousin, ain't he?"

Paulo nodded and smiled.

Doyle ignored Paulo's similar reaction to that of his cousin and barked, "Let's go then. I want to be heading toward Bolivia within the hour."

They were.

Doyle sat at the rear of the boat with the outboard motor throttle in one hand and a bottle of cachaça in the other. His straw hat was pulled down tight and over his head and his threadbare cotton shirt was open to the waist in order to better cool his heavy gut. Paulo and Angel sat at the bow and they waved to friends and family and even complete strangers who were on the river fishing, gathering water, or washing clothing as they passed.

The first hour out of Messias, the group passed three small boats of fishermen. Each was hugging the shore with their craft and pulling in gill nets dotted with piranha and freshwater barracuda. They passed a small settlement on the riverbank where they saw naked children playing alongside pigs and chickens. Settlements gave way to impenetrable jungle and both sides of the river soon became towering walls of green.

A pod of freshwater dolphins, their skin cadaverous pink in color, followed the boat for a time but quit the chase after a short period.

Sometime later they discovered an island of white gypsum that grew in the center of the river as the result of some heavy flooding. The island stood only a foot above the middle of the river and Paulo called that the channel to the east was better and it was until the water grew so shallow that Doyle had to raise the prop and the craft had to be pulled until deeper water once again presented itself. Shortly before sunset, Paulo sighted a small herd of capybara swimming across a narrow point in the river. Doyle sped into the herd of giant rats and the group panicked and swam at astonishing speeds in every direction, all the while bellowing in fright. Doyle brought the boat alongside a smaller animal and Paulo and Angel wrestled it into the boat then slit the animal's throat. The cub cried in fright and collapsed to the bottom of the boat and into an ever-growing pool of blood.

"Go on and clean it," Doyle yelled over the motor. "You already trashed the boat up there. Looks like ya' painted it in blood for Christ's sake."

The two Indians gutted the 30-pound rat and threw the intestines overboard and into the brown waters of the Rio Abuna. The expedition found a beach to camp on a half hour later and Paulo made a fire while Angel went into the jungle in search of more wood. He returned a short time later and quickly fashioned a cooking rack from several freshly cut limbs and laid it over the fire. The fire burned to coals and Paulo threw strips of capybara meat on the rack and watched as they cooked. Darkness fell and the three men sat around the fire gorging themselves on meat.

"No tomorrow. Day after," Paulo tried to explain. "We go to different river."

"Why?" Doyle questioned.

"Caruk Indian no like whites. Or us," Paulo paused to gesture to himself and his cousin.

Doyle nodded then thrust half a fist sized chunk of meat into his mouth. He partially chewed it then sought clarification.

"Day after tomorrow?" he asked.

"This day or to the day after or before," Paulo explained.

Doyle shook his head at Paulo's poor English and bellowed, "I never understand a God damn thing that comes outta your mouth. Just tell me when we get there."

11.

Blackie lived with his family in a small home on the outskirts of town. The house was built with mismatched wooden planks and a thatched roof crafted from found limbs. A half dead emaciated cat lay panting on the front porch and half a dozen chickens ambled throughout the packed earth yard. Blackie exited the house just as Barrett and Neal approached the porch.

Neal watched as Barrett and Blackie greeted one another. It was easy to see that the two men respected one another and shared a mutual history. Despite this, the two appeared worlds apart. Whereas Barrett was tall and lean, Blackie stood just a hair over five feet tall and was stout. His skin was extremely dark, almost the color of chocolate, and his eyes so brown as to be black.

"Neal," Barrett began. "This is Blackie, my assistant."

Neal stepped up on the porch and shook hands with Blackie. The three men sat upon a chair, crate, and a large stump that was used as a stool or chopping block.

"You bring me cigarettes?" Blackie asked of Barrett.

"No," Barrett answered. "I've been busy. I'll bring you plenty for the trip."

Blackie stood.

"We leave today?" he excitedly asked.

Barrett laughed then asked Blackie why he was in such a hurry to get on the river. Blackie explained that the past few weeks at home had been terrible. His wife and teenage daughter had been arguing about everything and each sought to get him on her side. Neal found this complaint humorous and laughed out loud.

"Why you laugh?" Blackie asked.

"Because that very thing was going on at my house when I left home. My wife and 15-year-old daughter can't seem to stand one another. They can't be in the same room without yelling at one another."

Blackie smiled at the realization that white men in America had the same problems as Manaus Indians in Brazil.

Neal used his story as a launchpad to explain to Blackie why he was in the Amazon. He told of the snake and of his desire to mount an expedition to where it was last sighted. He did not tell Blackie about Barrett going to jail or how he got him released. He guessed that, given Blackie's knowledge of Barrett, he would find the story anything out of the ordinary.

"I know Fawcett story," Blackie admitted in broken English. "I know the Mother of Waters. I believe."

Barrett shook his head in disbelief.

"What?" Blackie responded.

"You believe that crap? That a giant snake made the rivers of the Amazon?" Barrett laughed.

"Yes. I believe," Blackie assured him. "Stories that grow big always start small and from the true."

"I wholeheartedly agree," Neal interjected. "And could not have said it better."

"Getting there bad trouble," Blackie continued. "Karuk Indians no like whites. No like anyone. I no speak Karuk. You no speak Karuk."

"Forgot about them," Barrett said in exasperation.

"Can we go around their village?"

Blackie thought for a moment. Barrett lost patience in waiting.

"Well?!" he barked. "Can we go around them?"

"Hard to think when you no bring me cigarettes," Blackie laughed.

Barrett shook his head.

Neal smiled.

Blackie continued.

"In small boat? Yes. In your boat? No."

Barrett thought for a moment then instructed Blackie to put on two additional hands for the trip thinking that their presence would certainly help if they encountered the Karuk.

"That be good," Blackie agreed. "I use help."

Barrett nodded.

The three men sat on the deck of Blackie's home making plans for the next several hours. They discussed food, gear, travel distances, and precautions. Blackie said how many cigarettes he would need and Barrett laughed saying that he could have half of that. Barrett theorized the number of cigars he would need and Blackie scoffed and asked why Barrett should get more smokes than him. Barrett answered because he was the guy that decided if Blackie got paid or not and Blackie let the matter drop.

Barrett was discussing snake trapping methods when there came a sudden commotion from inside the house. The sound of two female voices yelling at one another echoed across the porch. Barrett stood and said with a smile, "Time to go. You have fun, Blackie."

Blackie bolted up in anger and begged, "We go soon, yes?"

12.

Ma Gert ran a supply store that primarily catered to ex-patriots and fishermen. Her store was located on the wharf and, despite Ma Gert being the sole employee, was open 24 hours a day. Some said this was because Ma Gert suffered from insomnia. A few local Indians believed this was because she was a witch. Barrett thought she was constantly awake because she was too damn mean to sleep.

"The Sandman don't want nothing to do with her and her shit," Barrett had once joked with Blackie.

Blackie thought on the matter then asked, "Is Sandman her husband? I no to meet."

Barrett thought of explaining the Sandman mythology to Blackie then thought the better of it and instead lit a cigar.

Barrett and Neal entered the small store to find it vacant of all customers and Ma Gert leaning on the makeshift counter smoking a hand rolled cigarette. She coughed at the sight of Barrett and barked through wrinkled lips, "You better be here to pay your bill and not to beg for credit."

"Relax Ma," Barrett oozed. He gestured behind him to Neal and continued, "I brought my banker."

Neal was caught off-guard by the introduction, knowing it to be false. He ambled forward with his hand held before him. "Dr. Neal Coldwell, American Museum of Natural History."

Ma Gert shot Neal's hand down with a stern look. She took a long drag on her cigarette and exhaled.

"So, you're the Doc. Grapevine said we had a scientist among us." Ma Gert raised a finger in Barrett's direction. "But you can't be that bright if you're hanging out with this guy."

"Now, Ma…" Barrett started.

Ma Gert raised her palm.

"Don't want to hear it. Not 'less starts with, 'Here's your money.'"

Neal took a step sideways and to in front of Ma Gert. Her face was tanned and lined from years of cigarette smoking and her gray ponytail was brittle and stiff. Neal could see that she was sitting on a stool but not any hint of her height or weight given the counter between them.

"I will be taking care of Mr. Walker's outstanding balance."

"Just like you did over there with our fair chief of police."

"You heard about that?" Neal asked in surprise.

"I hear about everything. And know about everything," Ma Gert explained. She looked across the store to Barrett. "Knew about you and the chief's wife from the first time it happened and even know that your buddy Doyle headed out yesterday after your snake."

Neal spun around in panic. He stared at Barrett with wild eyes and asked, "Doyle?"

"Don't worry about him," Barrett assured Neal. "He's the amateur hour. Won't get even halfway to where we're going before he gives up."

"I don't want to take that chance," Neal nervously stated.

"Then all the more reason to get our supplies and get on our way," Barrett countered.

Neal nodded and returned back to the store owner.

"Ma Gert?"

"Yes Doc."

"Seeing as you have your finger on the pulse of the community, I'm sure you have an idea where we're going and what we will be needing."

"If you have money I do."

"I have money."

Ma Gert ground her cigarette into the wooden countertop and stood from her stool. She knelt down behind the counter and out of sight then came up with pack after pack of cigarettes. She repeated the process several more times until the counter was tiled with cigarette packs.

"That ought to do Blackie for a month or so."

Neal smiled.

Barrett didn't.

He instead walked forward and lay his hands upon the counter.

"Now that Blackie is taken care of, let's get to business."

For the next hour, Ma Gert boxed a horde of supplies. She packed boxes of ammunition, bottles of cachaça, cigars, dry goods, and clothing. She bundled dozens of cheap machetes, canteens, and stick candy, cooking utensils, hardware, and deck shoes. She fitted

Neal in more jungle appropriate clothing and convinced him to carry a pistol and knife on his belt and to place a better hat upon his head. She added to the mix fishhooks of various sizes, line, crossbow bolts, and link after link of rope. She had just settled the bill when Blackie entered the store with two young Indians in tow.

"Take to boat?" Blackie asked of Barrett.

"How did you know we were finished?" Barrett asked.

"Grapevine," Ma Gert offered. "The grapevine."

13.

Barrett named his boat *Scout* after the ship that brought him to Brazil and his new life so many years ago. Built in the United Kingdom in 1915, Barrett's *Scout* was a 35-foot open hull wooden steamship that came to Brazil in order to ferry missionaries up-and-down Amazonia. The boat sank when it hit submerged debris in 1920. Barrett salvaged and rebuilt the boat over a period of six months. He had used the boat as his base of operations ever since.

Neal wasn't exactly impressed by the *Scout* nor was he disappointed. He had seen worse vessels - the one he had used in the Everglades years ago came to mind - and knew from experience that often the hardest looking implements were usually the best.

The boat was cluttered with gear and supplies, and Neal noticed that only the stern of the boat offered any protection from the elements in the form of a threadbare canvas awning. Neal assumed there was room for at least one or two people to sleep below deck but knowing what he did of tropical climates and the unexpected rain showers they often produced, he thought the area probably was reserved for storage of goods that couldn't get wet. There were two wooden canoes tied to the stern of the craft and each was loaded with supplies and carried a small outboard motor at its rear.

"Beautiful she ain't," Barrett admitted looking down on the craft. "But she's never let me down."

"Always first time," Blackie joked as he came up behind Barrett and Neal.

Blackie was followed by António and Lucas, the two hands he had hired for the expedition. They along with Blackie were carrying the last of the supplies from Ma Gert.

"*Scout* stand no chance against monster snake," Blackie continued.

"Snake won't come near the *Scout* if you're on it," Barrett joked back. "As bad as you smell."

Blackie smiled at the comment then directed António and Lucas to put their wares into the canoes closest to the shore.

Barrett watched this and stretched upward then grabbed his lower back in pain. He pulled a fresh cigar from his pocket, bit the end off and spat it into the river. He ignited a match by drawing it against his pistol, lit his cigar, and puffed away as he gazed at the river before him. The noonday sun was blazing upon the water and the air was thick with heavy humidity. He walked to the end of the wharf, dropped down into the *Scout*, checked the boiler, then looked to Blackie.

"What'cha say?" he asked.

Blackie looked upriver then to the sky above.

"We do good," Blackie replied.

Barrett stared up to Neal who still stood atop the dock.

"You ready?" Barrett asked.

"Now?"

"Yes, now," Barrett answered through a cloud of cigar smoke.

Neal had waited so long for this moment that he had a difficult time believing it had finally come. He was about to embark on the journey of a lifetime, one that if successful would enter his name into the annals of science forever. He had never felt so important.

Barrett ruined the moment with a directive.

"Come on Doc, move your ass."

Neal came back to reality and climbed aboard the *Scout*. António and Lucas climbed into the two canoes behind the boat and Blackie situated himself at the bow of the *Scout*. Ropes were cast off and Barrett opened the throttle. The *Scout* puffed slowly out toward the center of the river then sped forward and against the flow of water.

They passed the outskirts of town and saw children playing at the water's edge as well as folks tending to their boats or to their docks or the pilings that held them aloft. They passed a group of women who sat cleaning a pile of dead turtles and they waved with blood-soaked hands as the boat passed. Barrett settled into a sort of trance and ignored those he passed and instead concentrated on the river before him.

Neal's disposition was the opposite of Barrett's. Neal was hyper alert. He studied the river before the craft and the banks to either side. He noted the size and ethnicity of the people they passed and what activities they were engaged in. He studied the boats and homes they passed, the fields and how they were planted, and the crops that grew there. He noted the animals he saw along the shore, the dogs and cats, the pigs and chickens, the few horses, and one skeletal goat. When settlement gave way to jungle, he watched the trees and the birds that flew among them. He listened intently to the sounds that echoed from the forest and for any vocal response to their craft disturbing the river. He watched Blackie to see what, if anything, he took note of.

They had traveled just over two hours when Blackie approached Neal. He handed him a small fishing rod and motioned for him to take it. Neal did then watched as Blackie tossed a small brightly colored jig into the water. Neal watched the spool unwind. Blackie studied the line as it unspooled then clicked the release to stop the line. Blackie showed Neal that he was to pump his arm back and forth in quick succession so that some 15 to 20 yards of line away from the jig would jump and dart through the chop of the boat. Neal did as he was shown and roughly five minutes later the line jerked.

"Pull back. To reel," Blackie excitedly commanded.

Neal pulled back on the rod and reel as fast as his hands and wrists would allow. Whatever was at the other end of Neal's line fought violently and it cut through the *Scout's* wake in a frenzy of back-and-forth zig-zag motion. Neal smiled at the action and laughed as he reeled in the still fighting line. He watched the leader rise from the water then as Blackie reached over the edge of the boat and pulled aloft an oblong silvery fish the size of a small salad plate.

"Piranha," Blackie declared.

Neal reared back at the declaration. Blackie saw this and laughed. He removed the fish from the line and thrust it forward and toward Neal.

"No hurt. See," Blackie declared.

Blackie pulled the fish's lower jaw open to expose a mouthful of razor-sharp teeth. In them, Neal saw a type of savage beauty and the remembrance of every horrific story he had ever heard about the fish. He gave an uneasy smile then watched as Blackie tossed the fish into a wet burlap bag on the deck. Blackie tossed Neal's line back into the water and had him unspool the line until the jig was well past the canoes that trailed the *Scout*.

"For dinner," Blackie explained. "You catch 10, maybe 12 more."

Neal chuckled at the instructions then announced, "I'll do my best."

In less than an hour, Neal landed a total of 15 piranha. Most of these were small, weighing just two pounds or under but one, a black piranha, pushed the scale at over four pounds. Neal left his catch to Blackie and made his way to the stern and sat across from Barrett. Neal patted the gunwale and said, "She's nice."

"She'll do," Barrett countered.

"She'll do for now? Or until a certain time?" Neal asked.

"She'll do until she won't," Barrett replied.

Barrett stared ahead and to the river beyond.

"We're making good time," he announced. "We'll give it another couple hours then find a place to set up camp for the night."

"Sounds good," Neal agreed. "I think I got dinner covered."

"I saw that," Barrett commented. "Blackie made a piranha man out of you, huh?"

"That he did," Neal exclaimed. "I must confess, catching them wasn't all that difficult. But it was fun."

Barrett nodded his head in agreement and continued staring ahead.

They steamed forward another two hours encountering no one nor sign of anyone. They travelled through waters teeming with freshwater dolphins and past small islands of gypsum so white that they were blinding in the late afternoon sun. Upon these were an assortment of birds and Barrett explained that Blackie sometimes liked to collect bird eggs from the nests dug in the sand.

"What does he do with them?" Neal asked.

"Eats them."

Neal nodded.

They passed a swarm of bees so loud the group could hear them in the middle of the river and over the engine then passed through a section where the river narrowed and vines some 30 to 40 feet in length grew between the trees and over the river like some primordial latticework. The river widened again and before them stood a series of gypsum islands that dotted the river like step stones placed by giants. Something upon the shore of one of these islands caught Barrett's eye and he told Neal to hold the tiller straight. Neal did as he was told with apprehension then watched as Barrett hoisted an old rifle from a vertical gun rack next to the tiller. Barrett made his way to the bow of the boat and knelt. He placed the well rusted Winchester carbine against the gunwale and eased into it. He drew a bead on his quarry and squeezed the trigger. Thunder echoed across the river. Startled birds exploded from the jungle canopy and unseen monkeys screeched and howled. Some 70 yards away, four feet of caiman twisted and rolled on the sand, the upper half of its skull streaked outward and was painted across the gypsum in mediums of blood, hide, and brain matter.

Barrett jacked a new round into the rifle and ran to the stern of the boat. He took the tiller from Neal and opened the throttle. The boat sped ahead and Blackie stood at the ready at the bow. The *Scout* quickly closed the gap between it and the bank and Blackie jumped out and ran to the still writhing reptile. He rolled it onto its back and pulled it by the tail further up the beach. Barrett killed the engine then looked back to see that António and Lucas had already entered the shallow water and were making their way forward to secure the boat. Barrett jumped down to the beach and Neal followed. The two men rushed to Blackie's side.

"Even dead they go to river," Blackie explained. "You must hurry."

Neal nodded and knelt. He removed his hat and pushed back his sweat soaked hair then replaced his hat and gave his full attention to the dead crocodilian.

"*Caiman yacare*," Neal said of the creature's scientific name. "A fine specimen."

Barrett and Blackie watched as Neal fished a small retractable measuring tape from his pocket then pulled it the length of the animal and declared, "Four foot two inches long."

Blackie nodded in agreement as if he had known the exact length of the animal before it had been taped.

Neal looked up from his position on the sand and asked Barrett, "Is this average size for this area?"

"No," Barrett admitted. "Most of this type go six, maybe seven foot. I've taken a few ten footers but not many."

"This size taste best," Blackie declared. "Go good with your fish."

14.

Doyle coughed himself awake just before sunrise. He fell out of his hammock and hacked a huge wad of phlegm upon the jungle floor then rubbed his bloodshot eyes. He stretched upward then walked further into the jungle and to in between Paulo and Angel's hammocks. Doyle leaned against a large tree and urinated in the men's direction. Paulo sprang up at the sound of urine hitting dried leaves.

"That's right, Paulo," Doyle hacked. "The sound of my pissing means that you're late to get your butt up and out of bed."

Paulo bolted out of the hammock. He jumped to the jungle floor then kicked Angel's hammock. Angel awoke, climbed from his fabric cocoon, and joined Paulo.

"Y'all get it together and get to cooking," Doyle barked. "A man can't travel with an empty gut."

Paulo and Angel rushed to their duties and soon they and Doyle were eating the last of the capybara meat and drinking lukewarm coffee. They finished their dregs, climbed aboard Doyle's boat, and continued upriver.

The river widened and the jungle to the port side thinned and turned to marsh. Paulo pointed to a channel that meandered through the swamp and into the river proper. Doyle turned the boat into this offshoot, and they followed it through the lowlands and into thicker jungle once again. They traveled upon this narrow seam through the rainforest for more than five hours before it ran back into the Rio Abuna.

Doyle complained about the detour but Paulo assured him that it was best to avoid the Karuk Indians at all costs.

Doyle muttered, "Whatever" and continued onward.

A sudden thunderstorm burst upon them a short time later and it brought with it such heavy rain that Doyle steered his craft toward then under an overhang of thick vegetation to wait it out.

When it became apparent that they would be there for a time, Paulo took a small jar from his haversack and opened it. Doyle immediately gagged at the smell.

"What tha' bloody hell is that putrid shit?" Doyle barked over the driving rain.

Paulo ignored the complaint and instead took a treble hook from his tackle box and smeared the thick paste contents of the jar upon it. He tied a rusty bolt into the line some foot and a half above the hook and tossed the rig into the water. The rain poured upon them for another half hour. Doyle's clothes were soaked despite the protection from the vegetation above him and he shook violently as a chill ran up his spine.

Paulo's line jerked suddenly and he pulled back quickly to set the hook. The reel screamed and the line unspooled and Paulo set the drag and yanked back hard. He reeled in a frenzied motion and watched in pure elation as a blinding white fish belly broke the surface of the tea stained waters. The fish rolled and rolled exposing a black leathery hide and flaming red dorsal fin and tail. Angel fought his hand to inside the red-tail catfish's gills and pulled it into the boat. The 30-pound fish lumbered on the floor of the boat like some beached whale gasping for air. Its whiskers snaked back and forth in search of something familiar and its tail thrashed in an effort to propel it forward and away from harm. Paulo grinned at his catch then looked to Doyle for an acknowledgment that never came.

Instead Doyle complained about the journey thus far, about just how cold he had become, and the rain that was keeping him from making progress toward one massive payday. Another shiver shot up his spine and he shook then moaned, "This God damn trip is gonna be the death of me."

15.

They had been on the river for three days when they saw the first sign of the Karuk Indians. Barrett spotted a warning that they were entering the tribe's territory in the form of a painted human skull tied to a tree along the bank some 20 feet above the ground. The skull was colored in vivid red and yellow and its teeth painted black as coal. The warning was tied with strips of jaguar skin and a necklace of leather cord adorned with skulls of piranha, birds, snakes, and lizards.

"Why is it so high?" Neal asked in genuine interest.

"Water gets that high in the rainy season," Barrett explained.

Neal nodded and kept his gaze on the primal warning as they passed the macabre entity.

Blackie called to António and Lucas and had them climb from the canoes at the stern of the craft to aboard the *Scout*. Blackie went below and passed supplies from there to the two Indian assistants. Barrett slowed the *Scout* and kept his eyes to the starboard side. The jungle thinned then gave way to small fields and then to a vast opening. Small houses of limbs and thatch stood atop stilts and the small campfires outside each of these shrouded the village in an ashen haze. Twenty half naked men each with a bow notched and at the ready came from the smoke like apparitions from a dream. Neal watched this then watched the reaction of the men surrounding him. Barrett closed the throttle. Blackie held aloft fishing poles and lines. António and Lucas held before them a dozen machetes, their metal blades shining in the late afternoon sun.

"We no want you Christ!" one of the warriors called across the river.

"We bring gifts," Barrett called in return. "To ask for safe passage."

"No Christ!" the warrior replied in an even angrier tone.

"We have no Christ," Barrett assured. "Just gifts."

The leader of the group on shore said something to the others in his group and all lowered their bows but kept their arrows notched. They continued talking among themselves

"Come!" the lead warrior cried. He reiterated his command with a wave of his hand. "Come."

Barrett nodded and eased the throttle forward and steered the *Scout* toward shore.

Neal gave Barrett a look of concern and asked, "What should I do? How do I act?"

"Stay calm. Don't make any sudden movements. Let me do the talking."

Neal nodded.

Barrett continued. "And if things go south, taste bad."

Neal's face was ghost white.

"Taste bad?!" Neal gasped.

"Yeah. That way they won't want to eat all of you. At least not in one sitting."

Neal looked for some sign that Barrett was joking but saw none.

The *Scout* hit the shore and warriors encircled the bow of the boat. They kept their bows lowered but wore looks of heavy distrust upon their faces. The man who yelled across the river looked up to the wares Blackie, António, and Lucas held before them.

"We take all," the man demanded. "Give cigarettes us."

Barrett nodded and replied, "As many as you want."

Blackie's face dropped in disappointment, knowing that whatever cigarettes Barrett agreed to give the group would come from his provided supply.

"You!" The man pointed to Barrett. "Come down. All you."

Barrett stepped off the *Scout* and onto the shore. Blackie, António, and Lucas followed as did a very reluctant Neal.

"Me Juruá," the warrior introduced himself.

Barrett introduced himself and explained once more in sparse English that he wanted nothing from the Indians except for the ability to pass by their village in peace and for that they had brought gifts.

Juruá processed this then bid Barrett, his group, and their gifts, including "much cigarettes", to follow him. The group obliged and was flanked by bowmen on both sides as they traveled up the shore and to the center of the small village. They gathered around the central fire and soon all were surrounded by naked children of various ages and women who ranged in age from 19 to ancient. The younger of these were dressed in loose clothing while the elders wore loin cloths and stood naked from the waist up.

Barrett and his group stood at the center of attention with children laughing and pointing in their direction. Gifts were handed out and they passed from villager to villager to be admired or scrutinized.

Juruá nodded in thanks for the gifts then called past the crowd, "Yara!"

Barrett watched as the crowd parted and a young woman came from the village. She was beautiful with soft caramel skin and a wavy mane of brownish black hair. She wore a sleeveless cotton frock that barely contained her hourglass figure. She spoke to Juruá in their native tongue then walked to Barrett. He continued his study of her noting she was probably five foot seven inches tall and maybe in her early 20s.

"I am Yara," she almost purred. "I can translate for you."

Barrett stood stupefied. Yara was honestly the most beautiful creature he had ever seen. She was mesmerizing and he felt helpless in her gaze.

"What would you like me to tell Juruá?" Yara asked.

Barrett snapped from his trance.

"Uh…Tell Juruá we want to pass by his village and continue upriver. We offer gifts for that privilege."

Yara smiled and passed this information to Juruá and the two spoke for a moment. Yara nodded then returned to Barrett.

"Juruá asks where you are going and for what reason as he can offer you guides or porters if the need is there."

Barrett explained the goal of his expedition. He detailed the area they hoped to venture to and the quarry they sought. He explained Neal's position as a scientist and what he hoped to prove. Yara listened to this without a hint of emotion. She told Juruá everything Barrett had conveyed then listened as he responded.

"He says the area you hope to reach is very dangerous. There are tribes there that eat the flesh of men. Animals not known to man."

"What does he say of the snake we seek?" Neal interrupted.

"He said *Yacumama*, the Mother of the Waters, is known to live there. She and her many children."

Neal smiled at the news.

Yara returned to Barrett.

"Juruá says that I am to accompany you and that my presence is a gift to you."

"What?" Barrett coughed in disbelief.

"He says that I am to help you and that my knowledge of two worlds will help you."

"Two worlds?" Neal repeated.

"The white man's and that of the Karuk," Yara explained. "Juruá adds that as I know the land up to the area you seek, I am your only hope of reaching it."

Barrett thought of what to do and of what to say. Not accepting Yara as a gift would be an insult to Juruá and to the Karuk and could lead to serious problems. Accepting Yara would also lead to problems. The first and foremost of these would be his attraction to her and the problems that could lead to. He had yet to make a decision when Yara spoke again.

"Juruá wonders why you have yet to thank him for the gift of me."

"I was just thinking of the best way to thank him."

Barrett paused then continued.

"Tell him thank you and that we accept his gift with our whole heart."

16.

The Karuk prepared a feast that night to honor Barrett and his group and to wish their expedition success. The tribe cooked caiman and howler monkey, boiled turtle eggs and a variety of roots, and presented a multitude of fruits for the meal. These delicacies were eaten by all and around a great fire. Barrett and Juruá sat opposite one another and periodically nodded at each other with respect through the dancing flames. Yara sat to Barrett's right and explained to him who procured what food and the best way to offer thanks to each. Barrett complied with her suggestions but spent most of his time trying not to stare at her figure in the firelight.

Yara looked like no Indian Barrett had ever seen before. Her skin and features were Caucasian as was her almost statuesque height. Her curvaceous figure however was more reminiscent of Brazilian natives. Barrett sat admiring this combination of feminine attributes when Yara repeated, "This man says he has been to the area you seek."

Barrett came to.

He stared across the fire at the man Yara gestured toward. The man was much older than Barrett and his body was weathered by age and a life spent hunting the rainforest.

"His name is Caue," Yara continued.

Barrett nodded then asked through Yara for the man to share his story. The man did and Yara translated.

"Many seasons ago, I traveled through the area you seek with a white man named Fa-Set."

Neal almost exploded at the translated information.

Barrett quieted him and asked Yara to continue.

"I was a porter for this white man," Yara continued. "I was hired when I lived at the mission at Fortaliza Do Abuna."

Barrett nodded at knowing the town.

Yara continued.

"Where the Rio Abuna meets the Rio Negro, the jungle changes. The land grows dark and the trees cover the river and black out the sun."

"Ask him about the snake they encountered," Neal interrupted, unable to contain his excitement.

Barrett shot Neal a look of warning and Neal calmed himself the best he could. Yara asked the old man what Neal asked in her native tongue then recalled his words in English.

"The land held much wildlife; capybara, paca, sloths, and monkeys. It was a hunter's paradise and even a poor shot with a bow could feast on a daily basis. But the serpents that lived there were plenty as well. Many snakes. Most were larger than any I'd ever seen."

"Yara," Neal interrupted once more. "Please ask him about the monster snake Fawcett wrote about."

"I doubt he read the book," Barrett sarcastically countered.

Neal ignored Barrett's comment and continued.

"Fawcett wrote that they shot a huge snake more than 60 feet in length."

Yara thought of the best way to translate the enquiry. It took her a moment to decide the best way to translate the measurement of feet into something the old man would know then asked him about the snake. The old man listened then replied and Yara translated.

"He knows the serpent you speak of and says that its length can span the river. It attacked their lead canoe and was shot. It disappeared below the water but quickly rose from it unharmed. Fawcett wanted to capture the snake, but the men rebelled and fled the area saying that capturing the animal was not worth dying for."

Barrett lit a fresh cigar and offered on a puff of smoke, "Leaving that place was the smartest thing Fawcett ever did."

17.

Blackie ate the black howler meat in a state of pure bliss. Each pungent bite melted in his mouth and put a smile on his face that stretched from ear to ear. His enjoyment of the meat was so apparent that three of the elder women at the feast presented him with an entire leg of meat. Blackie thanked them extensively and took the leg into his hands and feasted upon it like a king with a turkey leg.

Blackie wolfed the meat from the leg then gnawed on the bone until its polished exterior glistened in the firelight. Blackie leaned back and allowed the food to settle in a state of euphoria.

This state was momentary though as he looked up to see most of the villagers smoking his cigarettes. He frowned at this then lit up one of his own. He sat enjoying his smoke, listening to Yara translate some old man's crazy ramblings about a snake the length of which spanned rivers.

Blackie believed in the legend of the snake.

He just didn't believe this old man.

Blackie watched Barrett's response to the crazy old man's story then half laughed at the childlike excitement that washed over the professor's face. Blackie thought the man was so excited about snakes that he would probably die happy having been killed by one.

Blackie turned his attention to Yara and to the way Barrett interacted with her. The poor man was taken with her. Barrett couldn't keep his eyes off of her and seemed to cling on her every word despite the fact that he obviously couldm't care less about what she was talking about. Not only that, but Barrett watched her lips form the words. He stared at her pout as if it was some type of fruit.

The old man finished his tale of the dangerous land and the hostile creatures he encountered there and those around the fire smoked and drank. Initially, Barrett and his group drank cachaça while the natives drank a potion made from fermented jungle fruits. The drinks soon changed hands however with all partaking in the two beverages. The group drank and smoked and laughed well into the night until the chief informed the group that day would break soon enough and it was time for all to retire, especially Barrett and his group as they would be traveling early the next day. Yara told Barrett she would spend her last night in the village with her family and that she would join him and the rest of the group in the morning. Barrett said he understood and watched as she walked away from the fire and towards the village.

Blackie eased next to Barrett and walked alongside him back down to the river and toward the *Scout*.

"You think she real Yara?" Blackie both laughed and warned.

Barrett stopped in his tracks. He puffed on his cigar and asked for clarification.

"You think she the real Yara? You act like she be it."

"You lost me," Barrett admitted.

Blackie laughed and told the story the best he could in his broken English.

Yara was the most beautiful woman in the world and could change her appearance to suit an individual's definition of such. Sometimes she was pale with red hair and green eyes. Other times she had skin the color of caramel and hair darker than the night. With some men she was tall and statuesque and with others she had full hips and a large bust. Yara used her beauty and her mesmerizing voice to lure men to the river. There, they would lose time longing for her, listening to her tell stories, or to her singing.

"Where's the downside to all this?" Barrett interjected. "Spending lots of time on the river with a gorgeous gal don't sound all that bad. And if she's that gorgeous, I'm sure there's gonna be more than staring at her and talking going on."

"You right," Blackie agreed. "She do more. She drown you. She eat you."

"What?" Barrett asked as if he hadn't heard Blackie clearly the first time.

Blackie explained that Yara was something of a mermaid. Although she appeared on land in complete human form, once she was in the water, her legs joined to become a tail. She used this along with her inhuman strength and ability to breathe underwater and to drag men to the bottom of the river and to their death. She left the dead there to rot and to become soft for days until she would return and eat them.

"She have spell on you," Blackie exclaimed. "I see it. She Yara. Same name even."

Barrett took another puff of his cigar.

"We'll see if she's that Yara if and when she eats me."

18.

Doyle's boat fought against the current presented by the confluence of the Rio Abuna and Rio Negro. The flow wasn't necessarily heavy or fast-moving but the boat's small engine made pushing against any current a difficult endeavor. Doyle cursed and spat and did all he could to maneuver the boat into the Rio Negro but in the end, it was easier for Paulo and Angel to pull the boat by rope up the convergence. Once into the Rio Negro proper, the men climbed aboard and rested as Doyle streamed them forward.

The river grew narrow and the banks higher and higher. The jungle fought against the separation by river and in some spots tree limbs from either side of the river joined in the middle. These became more and more common and soon the river was walled in a green arch that engulfed the sky. Day turned to twilight under the canopy and the heat and humidity grew to stifling proportions. It was just past noon when the men spotted forms of life usually seen only at night. Fireflies blinked in the thick tapestry that walled the river on either side and bats darted above them in a tornado of motion. Cries of birds and insects unseen came from the banks and sporadic vegetation rained down from high above to upon the boat and the dark waters that gave the river its namesake. The group traveled through this perpetual dusk for three hours before they came upon any place to beach their boat.

"There," Doyle barked over the engine. "Up ahead and starboard."

Paulo and Angel looked to the cut in the steep earthen bank that Doyle pointed to.

"Can we pull up there?" Doyle questioned.

Paulo and Angel studied the approaching beach. It was small but would provide enough space to beach their boat and to camp upon if need be.

"Yes. Go to there," Paulo bellowed.

Doyle motored the craft forward and onto the mud-slicked beach. Paulo and Angel tied the craft to an exposed root that jutted from the bank and Doyle stood and stretched. He made his way to the bow then dropped to the shore below and sunk up to his ankles in mud.

"God dammit alive," Doyle fumed.

Doyle tried to free himself but his girth was too much and the mud too deep. He looked up in anger and wonder at why Paulo and Angel weren't coming to his aid. Doyle searched the beach then saw the two men at the far end staring in horrified disbelief at something. Doyle fought the mud and after a time freed himself from the muck. He made his way across the beach, cursing in anger as he did so.

"I'm over there with my ass stuck like some beached whale," Doyle exaggerated.

Doyle's voice went dead at this sight. He stood staring at Paulo and Angel's source of amazement.

"Jesus Christ Almighty," Doyle exclaimed on the faintest of breaths.

The three men stared at the channel before them. The track was almost twice the width of the boat and half as deep as a grave.

"Is that?" Doyle began.

"Snake track," Paulo finished.

Doyle shook his head as if trying to wake from a dream.

"No," Doyle said matter of fact. "No. This has got to be something else. Snakes can't get this big."

"Yes. It snake track," Paulo warned again. "It true."

"Mother of the Waters," Angel mumbled.

"What'd he say?" Doyle harped.

"He say 'It Mother of the Waters,'" Paulo clarified. "*Yacumama*. The Mother of the Waters."

19.

Barrett, Yara, and Neal sat at the stern of the boat as the *Scout* plowed further upriver. It had been an uneventful morning and aside from Blackie, António, and Lucas catching more than a dozen piranha, the river had shown little in the way of activity.

Barrett asked Yara to take the till and she reluctantly did so. Barrett grabbed a bucket and rope from just outside the cabin and tossed it into the river. He pulled in the bucket hand over hand then poured its contents over his head. Yara chuckled at the unexpected action and Neal jokingly wondered aloud if it was bath time.

Barrett slicked his wet hair back with his hand, returned the bucket to where he got it, and took his place from Yara. Barrett noted Yara's smile at his action and joked, "What? I was hot."

The three watched the river for a time without saying a word. Barrett drove the boat forward, Yara stared straight ahead, and Neal took in everything around him with an unbridled enthusiasm. They remained this way for quite some time until Neal spoke.

"Yara, you speak such wonderful English. Where did you learn it?"

"At the mission."

Neal nodded then asked, "How long did you live there?"

"I was born there," Yara explained. "My father was a priest who came to our village to spread the word of God. He left when the village elders discovered he had gotten my mother pregnant. My mother went to the mission to have me."

"Is that why your village yelled they wanted no Christ at us upon our arrival?" Neal theorized.

"Yes. They do not trust missionaries."

Barrett lit a cigar and exclaimed, "Always a good policy in my experience."

Yara found the comment amusing and smiled then continued.

"My mother died when I was 10. My father two years ago. The mission closed soon after and I returned to the village."

Neal's face dropped at the pain Yara must've felt.

"I'm sorry," he offered. "I'm sorry for such loss."

Yara nodded.

Neal felt he should change the subject, but his curiosity continued to get the best of him.

"Why, if you don't mind my asking, were you made a gift to Barrett? Why on earth did they send you away from the village?"

Yara was not bothered by the question and answered it accordingly.

"The village found me a reminder of a bad time and treated me as such. Although I worked as hard, if not harder than others, I was mainly shunned. No one wanted much to do with me."

Barrett ran his eyes over Yara's body yet again and this time wondered how no one would want anything to do with her. The woman's curves were unreal and gravity had yet to find them.

"Well, I for one am very glad you are here," Neal cheerfully exclaimed. "I think you'll be of great help to our endeavor. I am especially envious of people like yourself."

Yara took on a puzzled look.

Neal offered an explanation.

"Someone like you, with a foot in two completely different worlds, I envy the knowledge and understanding you must possess. What a gift your parents' bonding gave to you."

A wave of relaxation washed over Yara. She was completely taken aback at such a beautiful compliment. She had never in her life felt so special. It was a very welcome change from the life she had previously known, one where she was made to feel as though her lineage was an abomination, unnatural, and proof of a false religion. She smiled at Neal and promised, "I will use this gift, as you call it, to help fulfill your dream to find the knowledge you seek."

20.

Doyle, Paulo, and Angel studied the snake track in quiet disbelief for another half hour. Paulo estimated the snake's length at over 40 feet and the age of the track at more than two days.

"It come from water," Paulo theorized. "Come to mud here. Then up bank."

Doyle studied the idea Paulo presented and asked again about the age of the track.

"Two days, you think?"

Paulo studied the track further then conferred with Angel for a time.

"Three day maybe," Paulo said returning his attention to Doyle.

Doyle nodded in thought. He stared up the steep bank that towered some 15 feet above the river then made his decision.

"We're moving on," Doyle announced. "This bank's too steep. A beast this big ain't looking to strain. He came out here for a reason but most likely prefers an easy transition from the land to the water."

Paulo nodded in agreement at the parts of Doyle's explanation he understood and made his way back to the boat. The three men climbed aboard and after much cussing, Doyle got the motor started and steered them further into the unknown. The air was still and heavy and smelled of rot and earth and loam. The steep banks on either side of the river subsided and gave way to partially flooded forest. The main river cut through this vast expanse and as they traveled through it, Doyle stared into the jungle in disbelief at its darkness. The canopy rose some 70 to 80 feet above them and appeared a solid mass of vegetation.

They traveled another hour until they came upon a rise of the earth large enough that would allow them to make camp. They beached the boat and tied it to a large tree. Paulo and Angel set up hammocks then searched the forest for the makings of a fire. They returned with tinder and kindling. Doyle took these and lit a fire as his two men returned to the forest to collect wood.

Doyle watched the fire and listened to it crackle, taking in the ever-growing darkness. A sense of unease grew within him at the place he found himself in. He, and so far as he knew Paulo and Angel, had never seen such a place. The landscape seemed almost alien. It was a relic from another time, a primordial ecosystem of perpetual twilight.

Paulo and Angel returned with armfuls of wood and they placed some of it upon the fire and watched as the flames grew to four feet in height. The three men sat watching as the fire gave way to coals and then cooked a few small piranha pulled from the river only hours earlier. Doyle told the men to build the fire up again and instructed that they should keep it that way for the remainder of the night.

"I ain't never seen a night as dark as this," Doyle complained. "It's black as tar under all these here trees."

Paulo nodded and stood. He went into the woods just outside of the firelight and cut two green limbs, each not much bigger than a broomstick and maybe four feet in length. He brought these back to the fire and handed one to Angel. For the next few minutes, the men worked the limbs into torches by splitting their ends open and into four prongs and spreading the prongs open and shoving them full of strips of bark and dried moss. They lit their torches and ventured into the flooded forest in search of more firewood.

Doyle watched as the two torches bounced through the darkness then into oblivion behind the trees where their glow was shielded by vegetation. Doyle pondered this then threw another log onto the fire. He stared out into the darkness once more in search of the torches but saw none and returned to the fire before him. He pulled his .45 revolver from the holster at his belt and checked to ensure it was loaded, knowing even before he did so that it was. He holstered the weapon and ran his hand over his stubbled face and listened to the fire crackle and hiss.

Small flickers of light darting through the darkness caught Doyle's eyes and he turned to see Paulo and Angel returning with armloads of wood. They approached the fire and dropped their wood in piles then restocked their torches with bark and the dried vegetation until the instruments burned bright once more.

"Another few loads like that should do us," Doyle exclaimed.

The men nodded and turned to face the jungle.

Their lights illuminated a scene of horror pulled from a child's darkest nightmare.

Paulo's mind barely registered the sight before it was upon him. Angel screamed in horror as half his friend's body disappeared into the serpent's gaping jaws. The snake reared back and Paulo's fallen torch illuminated his own legs kicking wildly as his upper body slid further into the demon's throat.

Doyle shook in unabated fear. He pulled his revolver and fired wildly in the serpent's direction. The second shot tore through the top of Angel's right ear. He howled in pain and grabbed the side of his bloody head and collapsed to his knees, screaming in agony. Doyle's last shot clipped the snake and the beast wretched back then exploded forward and toward Doyle. It took the obese boat captain into its coils and squeezed. Doyle heard his ribs crack then shatter and he screamed as the last of his breath was purged from his body.

Angel vaulted upward and ran towards the boat. The snake sensed the motion, dropped Doyle's almost liquefied body, and sprang forward. Angel ran past the boat and dove headfirst into the black river. He broke the surface and swam forward as fast as his body would allow.

21.

Barrett beached the *Scout* on a wide beautiful gypsum beach just below the convergence of the Rio Abuna and Rio Negro in the late afternoon. A camp with dining fly and several hammocks was set and a fire started. Folding chairs were placed around the fire for Barrett, Neal, and Yara while Blackie, António, and Lucas dragged a large log up to the area for the same purpose. Barrett pulled a tattered piece of cargo netting and a 12-gauge shotgun from the boat and told Neal that he was going hunting.

"For what?" Neal inquired.

"Anything," Barrett replied.

"I can help you," Yara offered.

Barrett replied with a look of doubt.

"I can make game calls," Yara explained. "Paca and capybara. I've often helped the village with hunting."

"Take her," Blackie offered Barrett with a friendly shove. "I make fish. You bring meat."

Barrett was about to say something to his smartass employee but was interrupted by Neal instead.

"I'd like to come along to see just how talented Yara is at calling animals."

"I don't think so," Barrett rebuked.

"Three's a crowd then I take it," Neal laughed.

"Only in hunting," Barrett replied.

Neal wasn't sure if the comment was a joke or not so he remained quiet.

Barrett nodded in Yara's direction and she followed him into the jungle.

They walked slowly and softly upon the narrow game trail that mazed through the dense rainforest. They passed through stands of trees covered in thorns and thick with ants and around trees so large they would not have been able to circle hands around them if they had tried. They hiked for more than half an hour until they came to a small clearing. Barrett unslung his shotgun and sat with his back against a tree choked with vines. Yara sat next to him and Barrett pulled the camo netting over them. They sat in total stillness for more than 10 minutes, allowing the jungle to return to its normalcy. Barrett stared ahead and through the netting, watching the jungle surrounding the opening for signs of movement. He tried not to give Yara any thought but it was difficult with her sitting as close to him as she was. He could feel her pressed against him to his left side, hear her breathing, and smell her. She smelled of flowers and citrus and he found the combination almost intoxicating.

Yara placed her hand on Barrett's thigh and gently squeezed. Barrett ignored the sensation of her touch and instead responded with a slight nod of his chin. Yara took a small leaf in between her thumbs and cupped her hands tightly then wet her lips. She raised her hands to her mouth and blew over the leaf and into the space between her thumbs. A faint shrill pierced the air and the sound shot outward and into the jungle. Yara repeated the sound several more times then paused and repeated the cry four more times. She paused again and this time waited until Barrett put his hand upon her thigh as instruction to begin once more. She made the call in quick succession five more times then smiled at the site of a paca cautiously entering the clearing.

It was a large male weighing probably seven pounds and sheened in a rust colored pillage. It had responded to the call of its kind and came from the forest in search of its source. The rodent eased forward, carefully surveying its surroundings for sign of trouble.

Barrett watched what he considered to be no more than a large tailless rat amble forward. He slowly raised the shotgun to his shoulder and pushed off the safety.

A sudden storm of black fell from the sky and upon the paca. The rodent squealed in fright and agony. Yara jerked in shock and crashed into Barrett. She clung to him in surprise and fear. Barrett pushed her off and fired. The shot caught the black jaguar in the shoulder and spun it around in a blur of motion. Barrett pumped another round into the 12-gauge and fired. The cat rolled over at the second shot, fought to stand, then collapsed. Barrett sprang up and handed the shotgun to a still trembling Yara who reluctantly took it. Barrett pulled his 1911 pistol and slowly approached the melanistic predator. He lowered his pistol in the direction of the cat's head then nudged it with his boot. The cat came to and bolted upwards in a flash of lightning. Barrett jumped back and fired. The .45 slug pierced the cat's throat and knocked it backward and to the ground where it clung to life for only a few seconds more. Barrett took a moment to allow his adrenaline to drop then holstered his pistol and returned to Yara. He held out his hand and she took it and he pulled her upward and toward him.

Yara trembled in fear and excitement. She exploded forward and to Barrett. She wrapped her arms around him and Barrett stood motionless in shock at the sudden hug. He embraced her trembling body and held it until she pulled away.

Yara's eyes filled with desire and fear, longing and need and locked on Barrett. The hunter saw this and moved to kill the moment so as not to interfere with the expedition at hand.

"That's one hell of a cat," Barrett exclaimed. "That hide will be worth a fortune."

The jaguar was a true monster, the apex predator of the rainforest. Barrett estimated that the beast weighed over 300 pounds and measured nearly seven feet in total length. But it was its coat that made it so unique. It was dark as pitch with even darker rosettes. The cat was an unexpected prize and one whose hide would bring a small fortune.

Yara held her hand to her chest and continued to breathe deeply in an attempt to calm herself. Barrett watched her chest heave up and down in rapid succession.

"I…I'm still in shock," Yara stammered.

"Yeah, I thought we were having rat for dinner," Barrett joked. "I guess that cat did too."

22.

Barrett and Yara returned to camp with the freshly killed rat and news of the black jaguar. Barrett sent Blackie, António, and Lucas into the jungle to retrieve the animal and they returned with the fleshed hide just as night fell. The group ate piranha and selected cuts of paca, both fried in lard, and drank cachaça and smoked. Barrett and Yara told and retold the story of the hunt and this prompted Neal and Blackie to tell adventurous stories from their past. Night rolled on and the group continued drinking and smoking and laughing and enjoying the cooler air that darkness brought. The expedition stared at the full moon and the sky full of stars above them and continued telling stories. The fire died down to coals and when they went cold, the group turned in for the night, each taking a hammock. Barrett had offered Yara a tent or the boat for the night, but she opted to take a hammock as well. Barrett honored her request but had Blackie set hers in trees far from the others for privacy.

Barrett awoke shortly after two with a strong desire to urinate. He climbed from his hammock and relieved himself against a tree. He finished then trained his ears on a distant sound.

It was water splashing.

The call was very gentle and almost dreamlike. Barrett took his pistol from his holster tied above his hammock and eased out of the trees and toward the river. He came to the edge of the vegetation and stared past the beach and to the water. His eyes fell on Yara bathing in the moonlight. She was naked and the water upon her skin glistened and shone in the starlight. Barrett watched as she fell back and into the water and floated upon the stillness of the river.

He thought to leave her to her privacy or to warn her of the dangers of the river at night but instead stood paralyzed by the beauty of her form. He stood transfixed by her flowing hair, toned abdomen, and her full breasts that rose above the water. Barrett's mind raced to Blackie's telling of the legend of Yara and Barrett thought perhaps the magnificence before him was some sort of siren and that her beauty existed solely to lure men to the water.

It was certainly working on him.

Barrett put the thought out of his head, gave Yara one more longing look, and returned to his hammock.

23.

Angel awoke with a start. He bolted up from the pile of leaves he found himself in and shook in fear beneath the jungle canopy. He circled around in a panic, looking for danger and waiting for the narrative of why he was where he was to return.

The image of the monstrous snake was the first memory to flash into his head. He recalled the serpent's enormous size, its eyes the color of midnight, its massive jaws, and how it had swallowed Paulo with such ease.

And seeming pleasure.

Angel recalled how fast the snake set upon Doyle and how it compressed his body into almost nothing in a matter of seconds. Angel remembered the serpent's speed and how it was on him and how he dove into the river and swam like a man possessed.

But how had he escaped?

Why, when he made it to the other side of the river, had the snake not come after him?

Angel's memories flashed through losing his sandals and knife in the river, scrambling through the flooded forest on bare feet, tripping on unseen roots again and again and how he had collapsed from exhaustion sometime late in the night. He had climbed to a high area and blanketed himself in leaves for warmth. His dreams had been filled with images of Paulo and Doyle's demise and the snake coming for him.

Then he awoke.

Angel surveyed his surroundings with fresh eyes and decided the best thing he could do would be to return to the river. As far as he knew, the boat was still intact and with a little luck he might get back to Messias alive and within a week's time. With his decision made, Angel gathered his composure and headed south.

The going was slow given the flooded nature of the forest and his lack of shoes. The fact that he was starving and the jungle so dark didn't help either.

He slogged through the just above ankle deep water, past trees tied in vines and dancing with ants and other insects. He fell into a sudden drop off that plunged him into waist high water and climbed out, utilizing sunken limbs and roots and by clawing through the mud. He caught a cicada that clung to a tree as if glued there and swallowed it whole after ripping the wings from its body. He choked on the taste and knelt to drink water from the forest floor. While hunched over he saw a forest crab burying itself in leaves at the base of a tree. He grabbed the crab and when it pinched him, he slammed it against a tree with a scream of surprise and pain. The crab exploded into a dozen shiny black pieces that fell to the forest floor. Angel picked up the two pinchers, cracked them further open with his teeth, and sucked the meat from them. He did the same to the main body and leaned over once more to cup water with his hands into his mouth until he had had his fill.

He continued walking south for what he guessed was hours. Although the sun was blocked by the dense jungle canopy above, he could tell by the growing heat that it was almost afternoon. He began to think he had traveled in the wrong direction or had somehow gotten turned around because he had yet to reach the river but then recalled that he wasn't sure how far he'd run in his panic the night before. He took a moment to collect himself and continued onward and through the maze of marsh before him. He finally reached the river an hour or two later but didn't see the beach where the snake attack had occurred. Angel looked up and down the river for any kind of sign but saw nothing he recognized. He found a small piece of earth above the water, sat upon it, and accepted the fact that he was hopelessly lost.

24.

Barrett easily captained the *Scout* through the small run of rapids at the convergence of the two rivers and up the Rio Negro. The journey was uneventful, and for the first few hours of the trip, the group saw little in the way of wildlife or anything out of the ordinary. Despite this, Neal was having a grand time as every minute brought him closer to the area Fawcett had apparently barely escaped from with his life. Neal thought of Fawcett and wondered if he was any closer to his desire. The correspondence that Neal received from him mentioned that he was in the midst of an expedition to find the Lost City of Z. Fawcett not only explained that the city was once home to an advanced civilization but that it had fallen to some calamity and that the jungle had consumed it.

Neal looked at the growing banks and the seemingly impenetrable jungle on either side of the river and thought it easy that a city could be hidden in such. Furthermore, Neal thought as Fawcett hadn't stated where he was going to look for the city, it could perhaps be in the vicinity of where Neal was now traveling. Perhaps, Neal's mind wandered into the fanciful, it was a giant snake that brought about the collapse of the City of Z. Neal continued these thoughts and watched as the banks grew steeper and steeper and how the labyrinth of roots and fallen trees visible within them seemed to be the only things keeping the earth from collapsing downward and into the river.

The river narrowed and the vegetation on either side of the river grew together and formed a tangled mass that blanketed out the sun. The *Scout* steamed ahead and into a time of dusk. Beneath this gray light, the group saw bats and flying foxes dart through the canopy in search of prey, fireflies swarm in illuminating sheets, and birds diving from dizzying heights into the water to retrieve fish. It was an ecosystem the likes of which none in the group had ever seen and all stared upon it in awe.

Except Barrett.

The fact that not even Yara had seen such a place bothered Barrett. The enclosed jungle felt purely claustrophobic and the lack of light was ghostly. The jungle that surrounded Barrett sent a slight shiver up his spine, a feeling of unease that he could neither explain nor understand.

Yara seemed to sense Barrett's unease and looked to comfort him. She stood next to him at the till and placed her hand upon his shoulder.

"What do you think, Captain?"

Barrett smirked at the attention.

"I think we're on a wild goose chase in the middle of nowhere."

"This is somewhere," Yara humorously countered.

Barrett fished a cigar from his pocket. Yara snapped it from his fingers and put it in her mouth. She bit off the end and spat the tip into the river. Barrett accepted Yara's flirtatious game and handed her a match. Yara took it, struck it against Barrett's pistol, then lit the cigar. She took a few puffs then handed it to Barrett who lodged it between his teeth. Barrett didn't understand Yara's sudden playfulness or the flirty attention she was bestowing upon him but liked it.

He liked her.

He lusted after her.

His thoughts on the matter however were interrupted by a sudden joyful excitement but from Neal.

"There's something up ahead!"

Barrett and Yara looked in the direction that Neal was pointing and Blackie, António, and Lucas stood in their respective long boats that were being dragged behind the *Scout*. They all gazed upon what was the first beach they'd seen in hours. As they got closer, Neal and Barrett took interest in the landing for different reasons.

"You must pull alongside there," Neal begged over the steam engine. "Please."

Barrett beached the *Scout* and all stepped onto the muddy bank.

"A boat beached here," Barrett said, gesturing to a shallow impression on the shore. "Not long ago either."

Neal ran ahead and up the bank.

Blackie studied the boat drag then reported to Barrett.

"Doyle's boat. Two days maybe."

Barrett nodded.

"Come!" Neal shouted. "Come! Look at this."

Barrett, Yara, Blackie, António, and Lucas made their way to Neal then stared at the shallow ditch he stood upon.

"This!" Neal exclaimed. "Is proof! This is a snake track!"

The group stared in disbelief at the track. The slide was enormous and the snake that had left it would have to have been gigantic.

Barrett looked to Blackie.

"What do you think?"

Blackie studied the track. He ran his eyes over the length of the shallow ditch, tracing it from the water, over the beach and up the bank.

"It snake," Blackie agreed. "Big snake."

"This is proof!" Neal almost exploded. "Proof, Barrett. Proof of Fawcett's discovery. I mean it may not be the same snake Fawcett encountered. That was quite some time ago. But it is at least as big as the one he encountered."

"You're right," Barrett agreed on a small puff of cigar smoke. "But right now, I'm wondering what happened to Doyle."

"Snake track much older," Blackie explained. "A few days older than boat."

"You can bet your bottom dollar that Doyle saw the track though," Barrett declared.

"Who is Doyle?" Yara asked.

Barrett explained who Doyle was and how he drunkenly eked out a living. He told of how he had heard that Doyle had set out for the Rio Negro in search of the same snake or snakes Neal was after. When Yara asked Barrett if Doyle was as good of a hunter and trapper as he was, Barrett answered with a smirk and the boast, "Nobody's as good me."

Both Yara and Blackie chuckled at this. Neal offered that Barrett had come highly recommended and that his abilities were highly regarded by most he spoke to.

Yara and Blackie found this to be equally funny and laughed even more.

Barrett accepted the ribbing then joined in the group as they assisted Neal in his study. They helped the professor obtain measurements, take pictures of the tracks, and to take a plaster cast of a small portion of the slide Neal felt the most pristine. The group waited as Neal took notes then insisted that he had all he needed and that it was time to continue upriver. The expedition loaded into the *Scout* and the two boats behind it and steamed forward.

It was late afternoon and the darkness beneath the trees grew darker still. They passed through a small pod of dolphins that raced alongside the boat and in its wake. The pink bleached creatures left just as quickly as they had appeared, leaving the boat and its passengers alone in the wilderness.

The afternoon grew darker still and the vale came alive with the sounds of frogs and the humming of insects. The air smelled of dank river and of the sweet perfume of flowers. The *Scout* had just rounded a bend when Blackie called from his boat. Barrett looked in Blackie's direction then turned to search what his friend was pointing at.

He saw Angel.

Barrett and his group brought Angel on board the *Scout* and tended to him the best they could. The man was haggard, covered in scratches, bruises and whelps from insect bites. He was missing half his ear and was famished and seemingly in a state of shock. He could say very little and could give only one or two word answers when asked about his situation and how it came to be. It was only after he had smoked two of Blackie's prized cigarettes that Angel calmed enough to tell his story.

Over a third cigarette, Angel told through Yara of his being hired by Doyle and Paulo to trap snakes along the Rio Negro. Angel told of their discovery of the track and how his group estimated the snake that had left it to be monstrous. Angel finished his cigarette, lit another, and told of the night Doyle and Paulo were killed.

Neal's eyes widened at the declaration. He eased closer to the shaken man so not to miss a word or inflexion despite the fact that his tale was being translated by Yara.

"It grows very dark here at night," Angel said through Yara. "Doyle had us build a large fire. The snake came from the darkness. It struck like lightning it was so fast. Doyle put one bullet in it, but it showed no effect. It swallowed Paulo whole then crushed Doyle in its coils."

"Ask him about the size. The coloring," Neal insisted.

Yara asked then translated.

"The snake had to be over 40 feet long. Maybe 50 or 60. It was big enough that it lifted Paulo from the ground with only its jaws. It crushed Doyle with ease. And he was a fat man."

Neal stood, astonished.

Barrett morbidly chuckled at the thought of Doyle's fat ass being squished.

"I couldn't see its exact coloring in the firelight but it's markings I could. It was an anaconda."

Blackie took Barrett aside and whispered to him all he knew of Angel. Blackie told how Angel had been kicked out of his own village for criminal acts and how he was shunned in most of Messias.

"I no trust him," Blackie added.

Barrett returned back to the group and spoke to Yara.

"Ask him," Barrett instructed. "If the snake was so fast, how'd he manage to get away?"

Yara was about to ask this but was interrupted by Neal addressing Barrett.

"You don't believe him?" Neal asked.

Barrett ran his hands over his growing stubble.

"I don't know," Barrett began. "Maybe he's telling the truth. He sure looks like he's been put through the ringer."

"The tracks we discovered earlier all but confirmed the snake's size," Neal continued.

Barrett nodded.

"But that track doesn't tell us if what Angel here is telling us is true or not."

Neal relaxed his stance then confessed, "Very true. I'm afraid I let my excitement get ahead of my duties as an impartial scientist. His story might be wrought with exaggeration. I'll make note of that in my journal."

Yara waited for Neal to jot down something in his notebook then continued her translation duties.

"I don't know how I got away from the snake," Angel confessed through Yara. "I did have a lead on it. Maybe the snake was tired from eating."

Neal interrupted.

"That could be a possibility. Snakes, most anyway, become sluggish after eating. It takes a great deal of effort for reptiles to digest food. In fact, snakes are quite vulnerable to predation after eating. In fact…"

"You've said 'in fact' twice in under a minute," Barrett annoyingly reported.

Neal laughed then continued.

"Yes. I did. Oh well, here goes the third time."

Barrett rolled his eyes.

Neal continued. "In fact…snakes will vomit any prey they've swallowed if they feel vulnerable. This allows them to flee or fight with full attention."

Barrett lit a fresh cigar.

"I don't see a 40 to 60 foot snake feeling threatened by anything."

Neal nodded.

Barrett quickly lost interest in Angel and in the professor's theorizing and announced that it was getting late. He explained that given the flooded nature of the forest, he decreed they should anchor the *Scout* in the center of the river for the night. The group could eat a cold meal then sleep onboard. Barrett set a schedule for watch with him taking the first shift. followed by Blackie then Neal. The group agreed and went their separate ways to prepare for the evening at hand.

"Listen," Barrett instructed, pulling Yara aside. "I want you to sleep down below tonight."

Yara started to object but was cut short by Barrett.

"Please," he asked. "Just sleep below. It's safer and, truth be told, a lot more comfortable than sleeping on deck."

"Truth be told," Yara chuckled.

Barrett didn't understand what was so funny and he let Yara know with a look.

"Truth be told," Yara explained. "Serves the same purpose grammatically as 'in fact,' the words you found so annoying coming from Neal earlier."

Barrett faked a laugh and said, "Enough grammar lessons for the night. Let's get some dinner."

Barrett started to walk away but was stopped short by Yara's hand on his arm.

"I'll sleep below tonight," Yara consented.

Barrett smiled and asked, "Is that a fact?"

Yara smiled in return and said, "In fact it is."

25.

Barrett awoke to the sight of Yara looking down at him. He rubbed his face and sat up in his hammock and took a moment for his eyes to adjust to the gray morning light of life under the thick jungle canopy.

"Wake up sleepy head," Yara played.

Barrett rubbed his hand over his stubbled face to further wake himself.

"What…Are you wearing my clothes?" Barrett asked in shock.

He ran his eyes up and over Yara. She was indeed wearing some of his clothing and she looked spectacular in them. Yara had rolled the cuffs of his trousers to accommodate the length and cinched them tight with a piece of cord. She had tied his button-down shirt tight just under her bust, leaving bare her toned midriff while her ample bosom spilled upward and almost out from the shallow neckline.

"Yes," Yara answered. "I hope you don't mind. I don't really have a lot to wear."

Barrett climbed from his hammock and stammered, "No... No that's fine. They look good on you. You do them justice…Gimme a minute though."

Yara watched as Barrett climbed below deck. She heard the sounds of rustling and rummaging then watched as Barrett climbed out of the hold with something tucked under his arm. He held out a leather belt holster. Yara reluctantly took the belt and pulled the pistol from inside its home. It was an old, worn revolver.

"It's a .38," Barrett explained. "You know how to use it?"

Yara nodded.

"Something wrong?" Barrett asked.

"No," Yara replied. "But why are you giving me this?"

"Cuz I want you to be safe."

Yara nodded.

"And cuz you're already wearing everything else that's mine. You might as well wear the gun too."

Yara smiled and holstered the pistol, putting the belt around her at the hips.

Barrett spun around to survey the *Scout*. He saw everyone up and about. Blackie, António, and Lucas were fishing and Neal was writing in his journal.

"Blackie!" Barrett yelled to his first mate. "I want us out here within the hour."

"Yes boss."

Blackie pulled in his line and together with António and Lucas they stoked the *Scout's* engine furnace and had the ship ready to head upriver in less than a half hour. They had traveled less than 45 minutes when they came across what was left of Doyle's boat.

Barrett beached the *Scout*, grabbed his shotgun, and hit the beach. The rest of his party followed.

Despite the fact that the small rise of earth was the place of two killings, all gazed upon it with awe and great curiosity.

All except Angel that is.

Angel walked along the small island in a state of near shock. Barrett noticed this and, after he had Angel show him where events had unfolded, sent him back to the *Scout* to wait for the rest of the party to return.

"What'cha think, Doc?" Barrett bellowed in Neal's direction.

The professor was kneeling on the ground, studying something neither Barrett nor anyone else could see. Neal rose and turned to the group and held out a dinner-sized plate of what appeared to be some sort of translucent leather.

"What is that?" Yara asked as the group moved to in front of Neal.

"Skin," Neal answered. "A very small section of snakeskin. My guess is the snake was about to molt."

"Molt?" Yara asked.

"Shed its skin," Neal explained. "I believe the snake had recently molted or was about to shed its skin. It's not unusual for the skin to come off in patches. Doyle's gunfire must've loosened a piece that was still affixed to the snake."

"How?" Barrett inquired, his voice dripping with sarcastic disbelief.

Neal paused to gather his thoughts, then explained.

"I don't think this Doyle person hit the snake dead on. I can find no blood. Perhaps he simply grazed the snake. This caused a muscle spasm in the affected area that sloughed off the skin."

Barrett accepted the hypothesis with a nod then lit a cigar.

Neal continued studying the area. He studied, photographed, and noted the snake's track, its size and depth. While he did this, Barrett and Blackie studied Doyle's boat to find it almost cracked in half. Blackie theorized that the massive snake had rushed over the boat and that its weight cracked the barely seaworthy anyway boat in half. The huge snake track in the mud before the boat backed up this theory.

"Take the fuel and anything else of value we can use," Barrett instructed Blackie before walking to Yara's side.

Yara was watching Neal prepare a plaster cast of a small section of the track when Barrett approached her. She turned to Barrett and asked, "Can you really catch something so large? So dangerous?"

Barrett puffed his cigar and boasted, "I can and I will."

Yara held her composure for only a second before she burst out laughing. Barrett smiled at Yara's reaction and allowed himself a short time to enjoy the moment.

The expedition got underway a short time after Neal finished his work. The *Scout* steamed slowly upriver and through the dark jungle. The river grew narrower and the vegetation that entangled above the river grew thicker and denser. Neal estimated the canopy above them could be 50 feet thick but no one seemed to find this of interest except Yara.

They passed below a small troop of monkeys numbering less than 20 that howled and screeched as the *Scout* came into view.

Barrett watched the black howlers' display and said aloud, "Makes me think of Selvagem."

"Selvagem?" Yara asked in confusion. "It means a savage."

"It's the name of the monkey that fights back in Messias," Barrett explained.

"Fight what? Where?" Yara asked in genuine confusion.

Barrett puffed the cigar lodged between his teeth and explained the monkey fights he attended at the Crying Messiah. He detailed the bar and the fights and how much money he had lost and won over the years betting on them. Yara listened intently, trying all the while to imagine such a cosmopolitan lifestyle.

"Messias ain't exactly cosmopolitan," Barrett laughed. "But it's a decent enough place."

Yara watched Barrett speak. She liked his confidence and his movements. She thought he was funny but also adventurous and inquisitive. She'd never met a man that made her feel the way she did toward him.

"Will you take me there?" Yara almost burst.

"Where?" Barrett shot back on a cloud of smoke.

"To the town. To that bar. To watch monkeys and dogs fight," Yara clipped at a rapid pace. "It sounds wonderful."

Barrett looked Yara up and down, taking notice of her every curve beneath his clothing. He smiled and promised, "Not dressed like that I won't."

Yara took the comment as a serious critique of the way she looked. Her face grew sad, then noticing Barrett's deadpan gaze, realized he was joking and burst into soft laughter. She play-slapped Barrett's muscular shoulder and almost cooed, "Then the first place I'll let you show me is a clothing store."

Barrett nodded and said, "Sounds like a plan."

The flirtatious moment was interrupted by Neal shouting.

"Light! Look up ahead! Light!"

All stared ahead to the river some half a mile before them. The canopy broke to reveal a blue sky shining down upon a land of waste. Both sides of the river were devastated. Dead trees burned black as tar and void of any branches stood like charcoal skeletons among piles of ash. It was a land of biblical destruction, a cauterized wasteland of char and ruin.

"What did this?" Neal pondered.

"Forest fire," Yara answered. "Started by lightning most likely."

Neal looked amazed. The idea of a forest fire in the rainforest had never occurred to him. He thought the vegetation would always be far too wet.

Barrett slowed the *Scout* then cursed the river before him. As was common in places that had been ravaged by fire, the flames had reduced everything but the largest of trees to ash. The rains that followed had washed away the ash and soil and unearthed the trees and sent what was left of the jungle into the river. Such had happened to the waterway before the *Scout*. The river was a labyrinth of logjams and islands of dead tangled trees.

Barrett dropped anchor and had Blackie climb aboard the *Scout* from his place in one of the two boats. Together they walked to the bow to assess the river before them.

"Maybe 20 feet," Blackie theorized about the width of the massive web of fallen trees that spanned the river.

Barrett nodded then added, "Good sized beach 25 or so yards past that."

"More logs past that," Blackie interrupted.

Barrett sucked on his stogie then belched smoke.

"Shit," he barked.

Barrett took another puff of smoke then relayed his orders to Blackie.

"I'll keep the *Scout* anchored here. You and the boys take the two smaller boats out there and cut us a path through. Make Angel help. We'll camp on the beach tonight and make plans in the morning."

Blackie nodded and went to work.

26.

Blackie collected António, Lucas, and a very reluctant Angel and had them assist him in gathering supplies from the *Scout*. They took rope and saws, hatchets, machetes, and an ax. During their time gathering equipment below deck, Angel discovered and took a bottle of cachaça from Barrett's supply. He rolled the bottle into a coil of rope then snuck it from the cabin and to a hiding place among his few things on board one of the canoes.

Blackie had the men load his canoe, untied it from the *Scout*, and motored to the logjam. The dam was massive and constructed by nature itself. Trees, limbs, vines, and vegetation all combined into a massive wall that spanned the river and stood above it in some places upwards of eight feet tall.

Blackie tied up to the lowest point of the bridge and climbed to the top of the mass of trees to see that the dam was wider in some spots than in others but fairly narrow near where he stood. He studied the tangle and surmised that he could cut a narrow channel into the dam that would allow the *Scout* to steam through. Cutting it would take some time as most of what needed to be cut was underwater. Still, Blackie thought, the job was doable. He was about to detail his plan to the men in the canoe below when a gleam of white caught his eye. He carefully walked over logs and brush toward what looked like a bleached piece of fabric stuck to a horizontal limb sticking upward from the dam. Blackie made it to the object to find it was just the top of an enormous snakeskin that had fallen down the backside of the dam through a maze of jutting lambs and into the water. Blackie stared at the skin in complete disbelief. The shed hide was enormous. It was maybe twice the length of the *Scout* and almost half as wide.

Blackie yelled to António in Portuguese to return to the *Scout* and let Barrett know that he and the professor were needed immediately. António did as instructed and soon both long boats were tied to the island of debris.

"Come. Look," Blackie called down to Barrett.

Barrett and Neal carefully climbed from their canoe and Yara followed. They crested the top of the dam then made their way log over log, limb over limb until they were at Blackie's side.

"My God in heaven," Neal almost wept at the sight of the skin.

"How old is that thing?" Barrett asked.

Neal ran his hands over the skin and declared that it could be no older than a day.

"Then whatever shed that thing's probably still within the vicinity," Barrett theorized.

"Probably," Neal offered. "Probably so. Snakes don't generally do much after shedding as the process can be quite strenuous and tiring."

"Then we've got time. Then let's get through this mess and to that beach," Barrett decreed. "We'll camp tonight and set traps first thing in the morning."

Blackie nodded and had his crew begin cutting the channel through the dam. Barrett and Yara helped Neal collect the skin and returned to the *Scout*. On board, Neal studied section after section of the skin, taking notes, measurements, and photographs.

It took Blackie and his crew more than four hours to cut through the dam and in that time the sky had gone from clear to the beginnings of the storm. Barrett gingerly steered the *Scout* through the dam and to the beach some 25 yards beyond it. He dropped anchor on the beach just as the first drops of rain began to fall. It was light at first but soon fell in blinding sheets that made setting up camp a difficult endeavor. Hammocks were strung in the trees at the edge of the beach and tarps were set over these to offer protection from the weather. A small fire was made and a dinner cooked and the fire abandoned to the rain. The weather broke and soon the night was still and heavy with humidity and held the promise of more rain to come. Barrett had the fire built up again so to provide at least some light and he made himself at home next to it, content to stand first watch.

Barrett's thoughts ran to Yara. He tried to imagine what she looked like when she slept, then thought of her bathing nude in the river, then thought it better not to think about her at all and to give his full concentration to guarding the camp instead.

It was a difficult thing to do.

27.

Angel stared up from his hammock and to the small patch of oilcloth tarp above it. The rain had stopped but he could still hear the heavy drops of water falling from the trees above onto the tarp above his face and to the jungle floor below him. He snuck another long drink of cachaça from the bottle at his side and let the heavy alcohol take him where it will.

He thought of Doyle and Paulo and how their lives had ended, of how this trip was originally planned to get him back on his feet financially, and how he had been kicked out of his village, and how that resulted in him living on the streets of Messias. These thoughts filled Angel with rage and he grew angrier and angrier at the world. He took another long drink of cachaça and thought on how life had mistreated him so. How he had been born unlucky and how almost everyone he had encountered in life had looked down on him for it. Angel's mind flooded to his very predicament as an example of such. He had escaped a monstrous snake only to be rescued by people that expected him to do slave work for no money. They'd made him catch fish, help maintain the *Scout*, and cut through a logjam. He didn't see the two white men having to do anything quite as arduous and he sure didn't see that princess, Yara, doing anything. She didn't do anything except sit there and look pretty.

And she was that.

She was the most beautiful woman he had ever seen.

She was like something out of a dream, a fantasy about the perfect woman.

Angel decided right then and there that he would have Yara. He deserved to have her.

Angel took another pull on the cachaça then quickly hid it away at the sound of someone approaching. The footsteps came closer, then to a stop, and were followed by directions from Barrett to António.

Angel listened to the discussion the best he could, then listened as Barrett left. Angel waited a moment then climbed from his hammock to face a very groggy António.

"What'd he say?" Angel asked in Portuguese.

"That it's my turn for watch," António groggily answered.

"Let me take it," Angel offered. "I can't sleep anyway."

António shrugged his shoulders in the darkness and handed Angel an old rusty carbine rifle.

"Thanks," António almost yawned as he climbed back into his hammock.

Angel carried the carbine and his half-empty bottle of cachaça through the maze of trees at the edge of the beach and to the campfire. He placed another log on the fire and watched as the flames danced around it looking for purchase.

The sky above was covered in a blanket of clouds that were only visible when distant flashes of lightning struck. The air was heavy and smelled of rain and of the river. Angel tossed another small log onto the fire and dropped the rifle to the sand. He took another long pull on his bottle of cachaça then ambled toward the half-beached *Scout*. It took him two tries to climb aboard and when he finally did make it up on deck, he tripped over himself and fell, almost smashing his bottle of cachaça in the process.

Angel sat in the dark for a moment to catch his breath. He took another drink of cachaça and ran his fingers through his hair, then stood. He made his way to the hold and opened the hatch. It took a moment for his eyes to adjust to the darkness of the makeshift cabin and when they did, he gazed upon Yara's sleeping form in a state of adulation.

Angel crawled into the narrow hatch on all fours and took Yara's left ankle in his hand. Yara's legs shook in sleep and Angel slid his hand up to her calf. Yara awoke in wild confusion. She pulled her leg inward then realized she wasn't alone. She screamed in fright and threw out her arms in defense. Angel panicked at the sound of her scream. He grabbed both Yara's wrists and pulled her from her makeshift bed and toward him. Yara struggled, fought, and thrashed about. Her forehead slammed into Angel's nose in the confusion and he dropped Yara from his grip, reached for his nose, and reared back in pain.

The boat suddenly shifted.

Clothing, gear, guns, and supplies crashed off shelves in the small storage cabin and rained down. Yara fell forward and toward the hatch. Angel fell backward and out of the hatchway and onto the deck. He looked upward to see a massive set of snake jaws descending down upon him. He thrust his arms up in an attempt to stop the terror from descending upon him but instead made it all the easier for the snake to consume him. The serpent took Angel in its jaws at the waist then reared back.

Yara watched in terror as Angel's legs kicked wildly, as his body slid down the serpent's maw. She saw the snake's throat bellow outward as Angel's arms punched inside the snake's throat in fight and heard the muffled cries of his agony.

Yara scrambled back into the cabin and over the fallen gear. She fought in the darkness to find something to use against the snake. Her best hope was to find the pistol Barrett gave her. She fought through the wreckage, feeling for anything that felt like the pistol. Her hand ran over something wooden with check lines and she grabbed it in her fist, turned and fired out the door.

Light exploded outward, painting everything in a shroud of bright white. Yara dropped what she now realized was a flare pistol and covered her eyes in blinding pain.

28.

Barrett ducked under the oilskin tarp that covered his hammock. He leaned the shotgun against a tree and eased into his hammock. He stayed fully dressed and kept his boots on, knowing that he could be called to action at any time during the night. Hopefully, Neal's theory that the snake would be sluggish after molting would prove true and Barrett could sleep uninterrupted through until the morning.

Barrett stretched out in his hammock and took a long pull off his flask. He listened to the rain fall from the jungle above and onto the tarp above him. Barrett could also hear what he thought was Blackie snoring.

Or maybe it was Neal.

Both of them snored like chainsaws and he had yet to be able to tell them apart in the dark.

Barrett took another drink, closed his flask, and tried to sleep. A short time later, a voice called him awake.

He sat up in his hammock and whispered, "Yara?"

The jungle didn't answer.

Barrett wondered if he dreamed of Yara calling him or perhaps imagined it.

"Barrett," the voice called once more.

Barrett was sure he heard it this time.

He could see his name coming off her parted lips in his mind.

But when he called in answer, he got no reply.

He climbed from his hammock in confusion and grabbed the shotgun. He traipsed through the jungle and toward the beach. He came upon the other hammocks and noticed António's leg hanging outward. Barrett angrily walked to the hammock and shook the hanging limb until António popped awake.

"You're supposed to be on watch!" Barrett cursed.

"Angel took my shift," António explained in a sleepy haze.

"Angel took your..."

Barrett's voice was interrupted by a muffled but shrill scream.

It was Yara, this time for sure.

Barrett exploded out of the trees and to the beach. He ran past the campfire then skidded to a stop at a sudden explosion of light from the *Scout*. He shielded his eyes then looked back to behold the sight of a monster thrown from the bowels of Hell. The gigantic snake lay half on the beach and half on the *Scout*, its massive head reared back and upwards of 15 feet above the boat's deck.

Barrett ran toward the dying light. He fired the 12-gauge four times in a row, its orange white flames streaking forward and into the darkness. In these spears of lights, Barrett watched as chunks of flesh and blood, shards of bone and scales exploded outward. The snake let loose an inhuman hiss of a scream that howled across the beach with hurricane force. The monstrous serpent shot forward and into the river. The rope that connected the

Scout to the two long boats caught on the snake's form and the three vessels flew forward and crashed into the steady current of the river. The serpent inadvertently towed the vessels further and further into the river. The rope snapped and the boats flew along the rain swollen current and toward the logjam.

Barrett tossed the empty 12-gauge aside and pulled his pistol. He ran to the water's edge and screamed into the darkness for Yara.

29.

The light subsided and Yara pulled her hands from her face to see the monstrous serpent reared back as if hit by the impact of the flare's illumination. A rapid thundering of gunfire cut across the river and the snake reared further back then vaulted forward and retched forth Angel's twisted lifeless form upon the deck. Yara screamed in fright and disgust at the slime covered cadaver. The snake spun around in a whirlwind and shot into the water. The *Scout* jerked forward and Yara fell out of the hatchway and to the deck next to Angel's remains.

The *Scout* sped forward.

Yara fought the slick fluid beneath her to stand. She saw the serpent's body plow through the water and felt the *Scout* being pulled in its wake. She rushed to the bow and dove into the black water. She breached the surface and swam towards the beach. Her arms hit the river bottom and she scrambled to her knees, then to her feet. She slogged forward, saw Barrett, and collapsed into his arms.

30.

"Blood and tissue. Some splinters of bone."

Neal stood from the scene upon the beach. He kept his lantern trained on the mosaic of carnage upon the gypsum sand.

"You definitely hit him."

"I know I hit him!" Barrett cursed through the rain. "The question is how much damage did I do?"

Neal studied the snake's remains upon the ground further.

"It's hurt. Badly. But given its size, I wouldn't say fatally."

Barrett's stare told Neal he wanted more information.

"Given its wounds and that Yara said it regurgitated its last meal and the speed at which it fled, I'd say it will hold up somewhere safe for a time in order to regain its strength. It's probably lying in the water resting somewhere."

"After it rests up, it's gonna be looking to replace its last meal," Barrett declared. "It knows we're here. And come morning, we're gonna be ready for it."

"I agree with your assessment," Neal offered.

"Blackie," Barrett began again.

"Yes boss."

"We set traps first thing in the morning."

Blackie nodded.

"We trap this thing, get the hell out of here, and make a fortune," Barrett continued.

Blackie continued nodding in agreement.

"I'll stand watch until then," Neal interrupted. He looked at his watch. "Dawn's in four hours. I'd like to continue studying these remains until then."

Barrett nodded and turned to António.

"You stand watch as well."

António nodded.

"I sorry," António confessed. "I let you down."

Barrett dipped his chin and warned, "Don't let it happen again."

Puzzlement washed over António's face.

"I no can do again," António explained. "Angel be dead."

Yara smiled at the comment and at António's naivety.

Barrett didn't.

"It's a good thing that piece of shit's dead," Barrett spat. "Otherwise I would have killed António myself."

Yara's smile widened at Barrett's promise of her protection.

Barrett told Blackie and Lucas to get some rest and reiterated to Neal and António to keep alert. All agreed and Barrett took Yara's hand and led her through the rain, into the trees and to his hammock beneath the tarp. The two ducked under the tarp and Barrett leaned the shotgun against the tree and took the flask from his pocket. He opened it and handed it to Yara who took a long pull to calm her still shot nerves. She offered thanks and handed the flask back to Barrett. He took it and took an even longer drink.

Barrett thought of what to say to Yara, how best to apologize for what had happened to her, and how he felt it was somehow his fault. A hundred different thoughts flooded his head and twisted about in a storm of anger and confusion.

Yara didn't know what Barrett was thinking. She only knew her thoughts and her feelings. She was frightened and relieved, felt safety and desire. Barrett had come for her. He alone had come to help her and here he stood before her in protection.

Yara undid the top button of her rain-soaked shirt. She undid the next button and then the one following and down the garment and then let it fall from her body. She undid the button on her pants and pushed them down her legs and to the jungle floor. She stepped out of them and stood naked and without shame before Barrett. She eased against him and to within his arms and kissed him deeply.

31.

Blackie climbed out of his hammock then roused Lucas from his. Dawn was breaking and the jungle was painted in an eerie yellowish haze. Rain continued to fall and thunder clapped in the distance. Blackie stood out from under the tarp and pooled rain in his hands then washed his face awake. He checked the knife at his belt then grabbed his machete and bid Lucas to follow him.

They walked from the edge of the trees across the beach and passed the dying campfire and to António. The three men stood ten yards from the river's edge, speaking in Portuguese.

"Anything?" Blackie asked.

António shook his head in the negative and explained that he had seen nothing all night other than rain and, "That crazy white man collecting snake guts."

Blackie and António laughed and looked across the beach to see Neal still studying and collecting the remains of Barrett's attack on the gigantic serpent. Neal apparently sensed the attention and looked up to Blackie and smiled.

Blackie smiled in return then looked over António and to the river. The waterway was swollen and the current steady.

The river suddenly exploded.

The monstrous anaconda drove forward from the depths, onto the beach and into the three men, knocking each of them to the ground. Blackie spun around and the snake dove at him and drove its four upper rows of needle-sharp teeth into Blackie's bare calf. Blackie howled in pain. António vaulted to his feet and thrust his rifle barrel toward the snake. The snake twisted and coiled, spinning the small Indian into a grip he could not escape. Blackie twisted over just in time to see the serpent exert such force on António that his eyes exploded out of their sockets and shot forth a distance of three feet. Blackie pulled his knife, sat up, and drove the blade into the snake's maw just behind its nostrils.

The snake jerked sideways and the blade snapped in two. Blackie tossed aside the knife handle and Lucas grabbed Blackie by the shoulders and pulled him forward with all his might. The snake jerked backwards and Blackie screamed in pain as his calf partially ripped from his leg. The snake opened its jaws and reared back in preparation to strike. Neal ran forward and fired his rifle at the hip. The bullet ricocheted just behind the snake's fist-sized eyes, sending scales and blood outward and through the air. Blackie grabbed his partially dislocated calf and held it to him as Lucas pulled him up the beach. Blackie looked behind him to see Barrett and Yara running toward them. Barrett drew his .45 and fired repeatedly as he ran toward the beast. The serpent turned toward the river and dove toward the depths. António's almost liquefied body fell to the ground and the snake disappeared beneath the dark waters.

Neal fought the lever of his rusted carbine then threw the rifle aside and rushed to Barrett, Yara, and Lucas who stood over a wailing Blackie.

"Hold it!" Barrett yelled over Blackie's screams and the driving rain. "Hold his leg!"

Neal reached into the melee and helped Lucas and Yara hold Blackie down. Barrett pulled his shirt off and cinched it tight around Blackie's partially destroyed limb. Neal rose from Blackie and pulled his belt from around his waist and thrust it into Barrett's hands. Barrett took it and cinched it as tight as he could three inches above Blackie's knee. Blackie's eyes rolled back in his head and he fell into unconsciousness. Yara shook Blackie and repeatedly called his name in an effort to wake him.

"He's okay," Neal snipped. "He simply passed out from the pain."

Yara ceased her cries and nodded in understanding.

"My pack," Neal directed at Yara. "Get it. I can scrape together materials from that to sew his leg."

Yara nodded once more and rose and ran across the beach to Neal's camp. She returned soon after and gave the pack to Neal. The professor dug through the bag until he found a needle and thread. He sewed Blackie's leg the best he could and together the group moved the wounded man back to his hammock.

"He needs rest," Neal explained. "He's lost a lot of blood. I'm surprised he's not in shock."

"He's one of the toughest men I know," Barrett exclaimed.

"We need to get him back to civilization as soon as we can. Time is of the essence."

"Yeah," Barrett mused. "But to do that we're gonna need the boats."

32.

"We should do something with the body," Yara said of António's destroyed form lying upon the beach.

The rain had ceased and the sun was fighting its way from behind the clouds. Flies had found the Indian's body and swarmed about it in the growing heat.

"We don't have time," Barrett exclaimed. He kept his eyes towards the logjam and to his boat stuck within it. The current had taken portions of the tangled trees and the dam no longer spanned the river. Rather it appeared as a large island of debris in the middle of the river.

"We've got to get to the boat before all that comes apart and sends everything I own downriver."

Neal stared across the 25-yard expanse from the beach to where the boat sat wedged among the trees. The *Scout* was partially submerged with her stern and most of her boiler underwater and one of the canoes was almost completely underwater. The group's only hope, as Neal saw it, was to somehow get to the other canoe that was lying upside down and wedged against the dam. The motor would take some work to get started given it being submerged but, again, appeared to be the group's best option.

"I think it best if we use rope," Neal exclaimed after fully assessing the situation.

"What?" Barrett asked.

"Your idea of swimming to the boats is fraught with problems," Neal continued.

Barrett turned to Neal as did Yara and Lucas.

"I think you should swim with a rope attached to your body," Neal explained. "If the current takes you and you pass by the boats, it could be dozens if not hundreds of yards before you could make it to shore. Then you'd have to walk all the way back just to try again."

Barrett gave the idea some thought.

Neal continued.

"With Lucas and I on the other end of the rope, we can ensure you won't go past the dam. And can even assist you in righting the boat if you tie the rope on."

Neal paused to point to the upside-down canoe. The current held it tight against the logs.

Barrett watched this and gave the idea more thought.

"I think you're right," Barrett admitted.

"No," Yara exploded. "No. That's suicide. Getting into that water. You don't know where that thing is."

"I know that if I don't go, Blackie dies and maybe us too," Barrett retorted. "We've got to get the boats."

"There's got to be a better way," Yara insisted.

"We thought it over and over," Barrett explained. "There is no other way. This is our only option."

Yara silently accepted this fact and watched as Barrett continued.

"We're gonna need a lot more rope."

Barrett led the group back to camp and together they salvaged cord from their hammocks, tarps, and packs. They tied these together to the few lengths of rope they did have and decided that what they'd fashioned would have to do.

Yara checked on Blackie once more. She wiped his brow then felt his head. She told Barrett that she feared he had a fever and Barrett responded by leading her and Neal back to the beach.

Lucas paused at the edge of the jungle to fell a tree trunk the size of his arm with his machete. He cut the trunk into a long pike some four feet long and carried this across the beach to where Barrett, Yara, and Neal stood at the edge of the beach. Lucas dug a small hole in the beach with his machete's tip and pounded the stake into the gypsum, angled away from the river. He tied the series of ropes to the base of the pole and handed the other end to Barrett. Yara took the rope from Barrett and tied it tight around his waist.

"I could've done that," Barrett mumbled.

"I can do it better," Yara answered.

Barrett turned to the river and studied the current. It was far slower than it had been earlier but still enough that it would present a challenge to his swim. Barrett decided to swim at an angle and into the current. Hopefully he could make it across far enough that the current would throw him into the logjam. If he missed, Neal and Lucas would pull him back to try again once more.

Barrett stepped to the edge of the beach. He removed his boots and shirt and handed Yara the 1911 at his belt.

"You're not taking this?" Yara asked in surprise.

Barrett nodded in the negative.

"Would weigh me down," Barrett explained. "Plus, I don't plan on being in the water that long."

"Good," Yara said before leaning in to kiss him. She pulled back and explained, "For luck."

Barrett saw the worry on Yara's face and sought to lift her spirits.

"Ya' don't need luck when you've got skill," Barrett offered with a straight face. "And I've got skill in spades."

Yara shook her head in disbelief then broke into laughter at Barrett's absurdity.

"Oh my God," Yara moaned before kissing Barrett once more.

Neal and Lucas grabbed the rope in their hands and Barrett walked into the water. The river was bathtub warm and the current almost non-existent that close to the beach. He shuffled forward in the tea-stained waters then jerked back at the sight of a freshwater stingray exploding from the river bottom just in front of him. The ray was black as pitch with vibrant yellow spots and flew on gently flapping wings.

Barrett guessed its circular body was more than seven feet across and the barbed tail that floated behind it nearly the same length. Barrett let the relatively harmless if undisturbed ray swim towards the depths.

Barrett dove forward and swam at an angle toward the logjam. The current wasn't nearly as bad as he expected but moved him in a hurried clip nonetheless. He swam hard and deliberately until a sudden blur of motion crossed the water before and beneath him. He stopped short in panic. The object shot by him once more, this time almost grazing his face.

It was a freshwater dolphin.

Even in the stained waters the animal's splotched pink skin was visible. A burst of black and green rose from the depths. It shot forth and took the dolphin in its mammoth jaws. The Cetacea's shriek of pain pierced the waters. Barrett thundered forward and swam towards the logjam with all his might. The anaconda's jaws snapped tight and the force exerted by the behemoth nearly broke the eight-foot dolphin in half. The serpent shook its head and maneuvered its prey headfirst into its jaws and began working it down its throat.

The snake rushed to the surface; the dolphin's ever disappearing tail snagged Barrett's rope and he shot backward at the waist. The force expelled the air from his body in a scream of bubbles. Barrett pulled the knife at his belt, cut the rope at his waist and vaulted forward and into a swim.

33.

Yara watched with great unease as Barrett entered the water. She had all but fallen in love with him, given herself to him even, and now he was risking his life for her and the group. She couldn't bear the thought of losing him. She watched as he dove into the water and swam forth. He swam in an angle and allowed the current to help propel him toward the logjam. Her eyes caught movement of a dorsal fin and she took the sighting of the dolphin as a good omen, knowing they wouldn't be in that section of the river if a predator was present.

Yara watched Barrett's strong stroke then turned to see Neal and Lucas letting the rope ease through their fingers with stoic purpose. The rope jerked forward. Neal and Lucas tried to hold tight. The rope burned through two layers of skin on Neal's hands and he screamed in agony.

Lucas wrapped the rope around his arm. Neal screamed, "No!" at the action. Lucas' arm was pulled forward with a loud pop as his shoulder dislocated. The driven anchor spike exploded from the sand and shot through the air and into Lucas' head. The blow knocked Lucas forward and atop of Neal. The two men fell in a heap on the ground and were pulled into the water as if shot from a cannon. Yara screamed as the two headed across the surface of the river then disappeared into the depths.

34.

Barrett hit the logjam and scrambled up a tangle of trees and limbs to the top as fast as he could. He spun around and gazed toward the beach and saw only Yara. He cupped his hands to yell to her but was cut short by a sudden explosion of debris 10 feet before him. The serpent's head sprang from the debris in a strobe of dark olive and matted yellow. It rose further until its head swayed some 18 feet above the dam. It opened its jaws to reveal four rows of glistening white razor-sharp teeth and hissed forth a thunderous cloud of rot and decay. The serpent reared back in preparation to strike. Its jaws opened wider and it shot its head forward and down at Barrett.

Barrett dove off the dam and into the water. He swam downward and into the tangle of submerged trees. The water behind him exploded in a storm of bubbles as the snake dove down and after him. Barrett swam further into the labyrinth of branches. The snake followed, the deep water muffling the sounds of limbs snapping into two or three pieces at the force of the monster's pursuit. Barrett pulled himself forward and in between two large tree trunks. He heard a heavy crash and felt the shockwave as the snake slammed into the trees. He turned to see the snake twisting and turning its car-sized head in an attempt to break into the underwater cage of trees he found himself in. Barrett looked up and around for an exit.

There wasn't one.

The trees and limbs protecting the pocket he was in were too thick.

He was trapped.

Barrett's lungs began to burn. His throat fought to open. His body cried out for air.

The snake battered at the two vertical trunks.

Barrett's lungs spasmed.

Burned.

He felt as if he would implode.

The fact that he was going to drown broke through his body's cry to survive at any cost. He had never been one to give up or accept defeat but now he knew he was done. He understood his life was winding down.

The logs parted as the snake pried its way inward.

Barrett flattened himself against the rear of his log-walled tomb and watched as one of the beast's fist-sized black eyes locked on him.

And then exploded at a sudden clap of thunder. The water was a cloud of crimson blood and membrane. The snake's head dropped downward releasing a scarlet plume trailing behind it.

34.

Neal was dizzy.

And choking on water.

He coughed and choked underwater. He fought himself into a ball and kicked off of Lucas' unconscious body with all his might. Neal righted himself and swam to the surface. He gasped for air in a frantic attempt to fill his lungs. He jerked his head around, looking for the snake, but saw nothing.

He felt the current pulling him and swam to the closest shore which was on the opposite side of the river from where he started.

He reached the shore and climbed from the river, utilizing exposed roots to scramble up the muddy bank. He turned to face the river and to hopefully catch a sight of Barrett or Yara.

He saw no one.

He grimaced in pain and from the excruciating throbbing in the palms of his hands.

He stared out again looking for signs of Barrett or Yara but saw no one.

And nothing.

Fear consumed his body.

Gone was the pain brought on by whiplash and the rope cutting through his skin, replaced by the realization that he had found his life's goal and that it had killed everyone but him.

And that he was alone and injured in an alien world from which he had little chance of escape.

35.

The red cloud of blood dissipated and Barrett beheld Yara lowering his 1911 pistol. He thought at first that she was simply a vision, some sort of dream. Perhaps he had already drowned and she was an angel sent to collect him.

Yara swam forward and offered her hand through the vise of tree trunks and pulled Barrett forward and out of the maze of trees and to the surface. Barrett screamed for breath. Yara put her arm around Barrett's chest and leaned him back and against her and swam to the shore.

They climbed from the river and onto a flat muddy bank only five yards past the dam. Barrett was still gasping for breath and Yara dropped the pistol to help him crawl forward. Yara stood and helped Barrett to his feet just as the river behind them exploded in a geyser of mud, water, blood and debris. The dinosaur-sized anaconda rose from the depths, its massive coiled body undulating and writhing forward in fury. The serpent jerked its head back, the remnants of its exploded eye dangling from its skull in red ribbons of flesh and scales, and spread its jaws wide to reveal a mouth of endless daggers painted in blood and viscera.

Yara pulled Barrett to her side in protection and together they watched in horror as the snake struck forward and toward them.

Thunder echoed across the river.

The snake's lower jaw exploded in a cloud of blood and teeth, flesh and bone. Another thunderclap boomed and the top of the snake's head blasted upward and back in a spray of blood and brain matter.

Yara and Barrett crouched and turned to see Blackie standing at the edge of the jungle with the shotgun at his shoulder. Blackie fired once more and the gun belched forth an orange spear of light that delivered another round of 12-gauge buckshot to the snake's head. Blackie fired once more, smiled at Barrett, then collapsed.

Barrett and Yara stood and jerked around to see the snake's massive, near headless form twitching with muscle spasms upon the mud. Barrett walked forward, grabbed his 1911 pistol from the beach, and shoved it into his waistband, then ran with Yara to Blackie's side.

The Indian was sweating with fever and obviously in a great deal of pain. His bandaged leg was bloody and his body trembling as if cold.

"Come on buddy. Wake up," Barrett said as he knelt over his friend.

Blackie forced his eyes on Barrett and attempted to smile further.

"Come on partner," Barrett joked. "I need your help skinning that beast."

Blackie looked over at Yara and smiled, then told Barrett, "I too tired from saving you ass. And…you have a new partner now."

Yara partially blushed and Barrett smirked.

"Yes, I do," Barrett continued.

Yara leaned over Blackie to kiss Barrett but was stopped short by his outward-held hand.

"No, baby," Barrett toyed. "You can kiss me after we skin that monster. That hide's worth a fortune!"

BARRETT WALKER WILL RETURN!

Gayne C. Young is the former Editor-in-Chief of *North American Hunter* and *North American Fisherman* - both part of *CBS Sports* -and a columnist for and feature contributor to Sporting Classics magazine. He is the author of *The Tunnel, Return to the Tunnel, Sumatra, Bug Hunt, And Monkeys Threw Crap At Me: Adventures In Hunting, Fishing, And Writing,* and numerous other titles. His screenplay, Eaters Of Men was optioned in 2010 by the Academy Award winning production company of Kopelson Entertainment.

In January 2011, Gayne C. Young became the first American outdoor writer to interview Russian Prime Minister, and former Russian President, Vladimir Putin.

CHECK OUT OTHER GREAT CRYPTID NOVELS

BIGFOOT WAR
by Eric S. Brown

Now a feature film from Origin Releasing. For the first time ever, all three core books of the Bigfoot War series have been collected into a single tome of Sasquatch Apocalypse horror. Remastered and reedited this book chronicles the original war between man and beast from the initial battles in Babblecreek through the apocalypse to the wastelands of a dark future world where Sasquatch reigns supreme and mankind struggles to survive. If you think you've experienced Bigfoot Horror before, think again. Bigfoot War sets the bar for the genre and will leave you praying that you never have to go into the woods again.

CRYPTID ZOO
by Gerry Griffiths

As a child, rare and unusual animals, especially cryptid creatures, always fascinated Carter Wilde.

Now that he's an eccentric billionaire and runs the largest conglomerate of high-tech companies all over the world, he can finally achieve his wildest dream of building the most incredible theme park ever conceived on the planet...CRYPTID ZOO.

Even though there have been apparent problems with the project, Wilde still decides to send some of his marketing employees and their families on a forced vacation to assess the theme park in preparation for Opening Day.

Nick Wells and his family are some of those chosen and are about to embark on what will become the most terror-filled weekend of their lives—praying they survive.

STEP RIGHT UP AND GET YOUR FREE PASS...

TO CRYPTID ZOO

CHECK OUT OTHER GREAT
CRYPTID NOVELS

SWAMP MONSTER MASSACRE
by Hunter Shea

The swamp belongs to them. Humans are only prey. Deep in the overgrown swamps of Florida, where humans rarely dare to enter, lives a race of creatures long thought to be only the stuff of legend. They walk upright but are stronger, taller and more brutal than any man. And when a small boat of tourists, held captive by a fleeing criminal, accidentally kills one of the swamp dwellers' young, the creatures are filled with a terrifyingly human emotion—a merciless lust for vengeance that will paint the trees red with blood.

TERROR MOUNTAIN
by Gerry Griffiths

When Marcus Pike inherits his grandfather's farm and moves his family out to the country, he has no idea there's an unholy terror running rampant about the mountainous farming community. Sheriff Avery Anderson has seen the heinous carnage and the mutilated bodies. He's also seen the giant footprints left in the snow—Bigfoot tracks. Meanwhile, Cole Wagner, and his wife, Kate, are prospecting their gold claim farther up the valley, unaware of the impending dangers lurking in the woods as an early winter storm sets in. Soon the snowy countryside will run red with blood on TERROR MOUNTAIN.

CHECK OUT OTHER GREAT CRYPTID NOVELS

RETURN TO DYATLOV PASS
by **J.H. Moncrieff**

In 1959, nine Russian students set off on a skiing expedition in the Ural Mountains. Their mutilated bodies were discovered weeks later. Their bizarre and unexplained deaths are one of the most enduring true mysteries of our time. Nearly sixty years later, podcast host Nat McPherson ventures into the same mountains with her team, determined to finally solve the mystery of the Dyatlov Pass incident. Her plans are thwarted on the first night, when two trackers from her group are brutally slaughtered. The team's guide, a superstitious man from a neighboring village, blames the killings on yetis, but no one believes him. As members of Nat's team die one by one, she must figure out if there's a murderer in their midst—or something even worse—before history repeats itself and her group becomes another casualty of the infamous Dead Mountain.

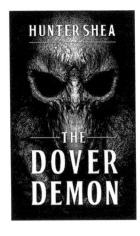

DOVER DEMON
by **Hunter Shea**

The Dover Demon is real...and it has returned. In 1977, Sam Brogna and his friends came upon a terrifying, alien creature on a deserted country road. What they witnessed was so bizarre, so chilling, they swore their silence. But their lives were changed forever. Decades later, the town of Dover has been hit by a massive blizzard. Sam's son, Nicky, is drawn to search for the infamous cryptid, only to disappear into the bowels of a secret underground lair. The Dover Demon is far deadlier than anyone could have believed. And there are many of them. Can Sam and his reunited friends rescue Nicky and battle a race of creatures so powerful, so sinister, that history itself has been shaped by their secretive presence?

Printed in Great Britain
by Amazon

56969282R00085